SHOOT
THE WOMAN
FIRST

SHOOT
THE WOMAN
FIRST

Wallace Stroby

Minotaur Books

New York

SHOOT THE WOMAN FIRST. Copyright © 2013 by Wallace Stroby. All rights reserved. Printed in the United States of America. For information, address St. Martin's Press, 175 Fifth Avenue, New York, N.Y. 10010.

www.minotaurbooks.com

The Library of Congress Cataloging-in-Publication Data is available upon request.

ISBN 978-1-250-00038-5 (hardcover)
ISBN 978-1-250-02247-9 (e-book)

Minotaur books may be purchased for educational, business, or promotional use. For information on bulk purchases, please contact Macmillan Corporate and Premium Sales Department at 1-800-221-7945, extension 5442, or write specialmarkets@macmillan.com.

First Edition: December 2013

10 9 8 7 6 5 4 3 2 1

For Dutch Leonard,
who set the bar so high for the rest of us

SHOOT
THE WOMAN
FIRST

ONE

Four hours after she got off the plane in Detroit, Crissa was parked on a downtown street, watching a rust-eaten Subaru with half a million dollars in the trunk.

"You sure that's it?" she said.

Charlie Glass, the one who'd brought her into it, said, "That's it," and gave her the binoculars. He was behind the wheel, Crissa riding shotgun. They were in a stolen RAV4 with smoked windows, parked two blocks down from the Subaru, on the same side of the street.

From behind her, Larry Black said, "Taking a chance, aren't they? Leaving it out there like that?"

Beside him, Cordell, Glass's cousin, and the only one she didn't know, said, "Nobody's got the balls to touch it. Marquis know that."

Through the binoculars, she could see the black and red

Tigers cap on the rear deck, where Cordell had said it would be. A half block behind the Subaru, on the opposite side of the street, a black Nissan Armada with tinted glass sat at the curb.

"How many in there?" she said.

"Three usually," Cordell said. "Sometimes four. Getting sloppy, though. Marquis caught them getting their smoke on in there last month. He rolled up with Damien to check on them. Whole ride smelled of reefer. He had Damien put a beating on them for that."

"Who's Damien?" she said.

"His brother. A couple years younger. He's the muscle."

She looked at her watch. Almost five on a Saturday, but only a handful of cars had passed in the half hour they'd been here. This was a business area once, sandstone office buildings and a bank, a row of stores. Now the bank was a discount furniture showroom, and most of the storefront windows were plywooded over, or covered by riot gates scrawled with graffiti. A barber pole hung drunkenly beside a doorway, all the glass gone. No one on the street at all.

She lowered the binoculars. "This is no good. Staying out here too long."

"Thought you'd want to see the setup," Cordell said. "So you'd know I wasn't lying. This might be the last chance for a while."

Fifteen minutes ago, they'd watched the Subaru pull up. The driver, a black man with dreadlocks, had gotten out, locked the car, and started walking. A Honda Accord had picked him up a block away and driven off. Almost on cue, the Armada had appeared from a side street, taken up its station.

She turned to hand the binoculars to Larry, took a better look at Cordell. Close-trimmed hair, round gold-framed glasses, denim jacket over a tie-dyed Bob Marley T-shirt. He looked like a college student.

"How often do they switch cars?" she said.

"Every time," Cordell said. "Different hour, different street. But that Tigers cap is always there. That's how they know."

Larry was looking at the Subaru now, resting the binoculars on the seat back. "Just the Armada?" he said. "They don't put anyone in one of those stores around there, cut a hole in the plywood, keep a lookout?"

"Guess he figures with those boys on watch, he doesn't need to," Cordell said. "They been doing this no sweat for over a month now."

Glass looked at her, said, "What do you think?"

He was tall and dark-skinned, scalp shaved clean. She'd worked with him once before, a takeover at a check-cashing store in Pittsburgh two years back. The take had been weak, but he'd been solid, dependable. When he'd contacted her about possible work in Michigan, she'd agreed to fly up, meet with him, take a look.

"Not sure yet," she said.

Larry lowered the binoculars. "What do they carry in there?" The oldest of them, he was from Kentucky, had a faint accent that drifted in and out. Early fifties, but fit, pale blue eyes, black hair swept back and showing gray.

"They go heavy," Cordell said. "Shotguns, MP5, an AK

maybe. There to scare the gangbangers away, is all. Shit was crazy here the last couple years. Dodge City, for real. Even an OG like Marquis has to watch his back. These young'uns don't care who he is."

"This Damien," she said. "He ever in there?"

"No, Marquis keeps him close. He's the palace guard. Never strays too far from the king."

Larry passed the binoculars back to her.

"I don't know," he said. "Seems a little careless, considering the kind of money supposed to be in there."

"Not careless," Cordell said. "Confident."

She half-turned in her seat. "All these stores out of business?"

"Yeah," Cordell said. "The whole block, except for the furniture place."

They heard a siren. She saw a blue and white Detroit PD cruiser coming up behind them, rollers flashing. Her stomach tightened.

The cruiser went by without slowing, past the Armada, past the Subaru. At the intersection, it braked, then turned left against the light.

She exhaled. Larry took out a stick of Juicy Fruit, peeled away the wrapper, folded the gum into his mouth.

"How do they get the car back?" she said.

"Same way on the other end," Cordell said. "They take the money out, put the product in, park the car somewhere, make a call. Marquis sends someone to get it. Then they junk the car afterward. That's why they always use a hooptie."

"A what?" Larry said.

"A hooptie. A piece of shit. That way, it's parked there, it doesn't stick out. And nobody drives by, wants to steal it, either."

"This the way it always is around here?" Larry said. "This empty?"

"On weekends, yeah," Cordell said. "During the week, there's more people around. There's some office buildings back that way. But on weekends, or after dark, it's like this."

"He's right," Glass said. "I've been in this town two weeks. It makes the 'Burgh look like Times Square."

She looked up at the buildings, a pale moon already showing in the afternoon sky. In the far distance, half hidden by other buildings, the gleaming glass columns of the Renaissance Center caught the last of the sun off the river. But this block was hard-stone, Depression-era architecture, dates carved into cornerstones. Empty windows, dark doorways. Ghost town. Deadtown. She pictured the vacant spaces inside the buildings, trash-strewn floors, broken glass.

"How long should we wait?" Larry said, and, as if in answer, a dark-blue Camry drove past. It slowed near the Armada, then again near the Subaru, stopped at the intersection. When the light changed, it made a left, the same direction the cruiser had gone.

They watched in silence. Two minutes later, a man came around the corner, not hurrying. She raised the binoculars. He was light-skinned, Hispanic, wore an olive-drab army jacket. He crossed the street, unlocked the Subaru, got in. After a moment, dark exhaust coughed from the tailpipe. The car pulled away, made a right at the intersection. The Armada waited, then pulled out after it, made the turn in the Subaru's wake.

"They're waiting to see if anyone's following," Cordell said. "They'll stay with it a few blocks, then turn around, go home."

The street was empty now. A scrap of newspaper blew across the lanes, flattened against a riot gate.

"It looks too easy," Larry said.

"It is easy," Cordell said. "But it won't be for long. This a temporary thing, with his new connect. They may change it up next time, do something else entirely. But right now, like I said, they sloppy."

To Crissa, Glass said, "Should we follow them, see where they go?"

She shook her head. "No need. If we do it, we'll do it right here, on the street, before they get moving. Let's sit a few minutes. See if anyone else comes out of the woodwork."

The sun was slipping behind the buildings now, the street falling into shadow.

"Has to be a smarter way to move that much money," Larry said. "Out in the open like this, doesn't make much sense."

"Like I said, it's temporary," Cordell said. "He heard that was the way Nicky Barnes used to do it, up in Harlem. That's his idol."

"Nicky Barnes is in prison," she said.

"Not anymore," Cordell said. "He's in the program now. He went and testified against all those boys used to work for him, the Council. That was his revenge, because they disrespected him when he was in prison, went behind his back."

"Bullshit," Larry said. "A rat's a rat."

"Who does the driving on this end?" she said. "For the drop-off?"

"Just some low-level boys," Cordell said. "Nobody he'd miss if they got arrested. Nobody who'd know anything worth telling the police, either."

"None of them been tempted to just keep driving?" she said. "Head south, keep all that cash themselves?"

"What I'd do," Larry said.

"They're too scared," Cordell said. "Marquis would find them sooner or later."

"Tell the story," Glass said. "One you told me."

"Couple years back," Cordell said, "a bagman took off with ten grand. Damien tracked him down in Cleveland a month later. Put two in his head, did the girl he was with, too. But first Damien cut off his dick and made him eat it. Just for ten grand. Word got around."

"Sounds like street bullshit," she said. "To keep the troops in line."

"Maybe," Cordell said. "Maybe not."

"How many people know in advance where the drop-off's going to be?"

"Five, six. Shit needs to get organized, people need to be told what to do, where to be. No way he can keep it a secret."

"That five or six includes you, right?"

"Has to. I find the drivers, that's my job."

"So if his money gets taken, you're a suspect."

"Maybe."

"Likely."

"We talked about that," Glass said. "There's no way around it."

"I won't be here to find out anyway," Cordell said. "Soon as we do this . . ."

"If we do this," she said.

"*If* we do this, I'll be long gone afterward."

"What about Damien?" Larry said. "Thought you said if someone ripped him off, they'd get found eventually?"

"Marquis headed for a fall," Cordell said. "It's just a matter of time. His connect got busted a while back, that's why he's buying from the Mexicans now, doing these hand-offs. Chances are his old connect is going to roll on him. Marquis an easy target. Word is, DEA been looking at him for a long time."

"When's the next drop-off?" she said.

"Next week. Don't know what day yet."

"He's moving that much product?" Larry said. "Half a mil a week?"

"He's stocking up, in case it goes dry again," Cordell said. "He needs to keep the cash coming in. He owes money to the Mexicans, too, for what he already bought on commission. So he's padding the bag a little each week until he's caught up."

"Five hundred thousand sounds high," she said. "You see the money before it's packed?"

"Nah, they do that up in the office. Behind closed doors. No one in there but Marquis and Damien, and this boy they call Metro that does the counting."

She was wondering how much of it was street talk, Glass taken in by Cordell's story. Cordell looked too young, soft, to be in the Game in any real way. But the drop-off and pickup had gone as he said they would. And even a quarter million might make it worth doing.

"How far in advance do you know the location?" she said.

"Couple days, maybe."

"Not much time. Who picks the spot?"

"Marquis talks to the Mexicans. They work it out between them."

"I know how it sounds," Glass said. "But Cordell's right. This is sloppy right now, because they're fat and lazy. That'll change. We got a window of time here. They may get their shit squared away at some point in the future. It won't be so easy."

"Body armor," Larry said.

She turned to him. "What?"

"I'm just saying. If we do this—on the street, like this—we need body armor, vests. Any of the rollos in that Armada start popping off at us with that kind of hardware, stoned or not, I want some protection."

"Good idea," Glass said. "I can handle that."

"You financing?" she said.

"Much as I need to. I'll take it back off the top."

"That a good idea?"

"You worried I'll want more say in how we do it?"

"Should I be?"

"No. Just thought it would be easier that way, for me to put out the money up front, given the time factor. That's all."

He was right. And aside from the body armor, they might be able to do it with minimal expense. She was looking at the spot where the Subaru had been parked, thinking it through, considering the angles.

"Well?" Glass said.

"We're good for now," she said. "Drop me back at the hotel. We'll talk tonight. I have some ideas."

"You thinking it's doable?" he said.

"At the moment," she said, "I'm just thinking."

"That's good enough for me," Glass said, and started the engine.

TWO

She always chose airport hotels. In a strange city, looking into possible work, it made it easier, quicker to get away if things went sour.

She had registered as Linda Hendryx, the name on her New Jersey driver's license and credit cards. Over the previous year, she'd bought two other sets of documents as well, in different names. She kept them for emergencies, each with a U.S. passport if she had to leave the country. The two sets had cost her seventy-five thousand each, but she'd been flush from her previous work. She and a partner had turned up more than two million in cash that had been stashed away for years, proceeds from a 1978 robbery. They'd taken the money, split it down the middle. It was more than she'd ever made from a single job before.

Glass had dropped her off first. She'd showered, dressed,

had a steak in the hotel restaurant. The waiter had just brought a second cup of coffee, left the check, when she looked up and saw Larry in the doorway, wearing a leather coat over a turtleneck sweater. He'd driven over from his own hotel, a few miles away. She looked at her watch. Nine P.M. He was right on time.

She got her own leather off the back of the chair, left cash for the bill and tip. They walked through the lobby together, out the revolving door to where his rental Ford was parked at the curb. She hadn't rented a car here, wouldn't. It made things simpler, reduced the paper trail.

She took thin leather gloves from her pocket, pulled them on.

"Cold?" he said. Early September, and Indian summer was starting to give way to fall here. Back in New Jersey, it was still in the seventies.

"No."

"Got it. Being careful. Can't blame you."

They got in the car. As they pulled away, a chime began to sound.

"That's you," he said. She pulled the safety belt across, clicked it into place.

"How long have you been in town?" she said.

"Got here yesterday. I'll go home tomorrow if I don't like what I hear tonight."

A plane emerged from the clouds, passed over them, landing lights flashing.

"What's your feeling so far?" he said.

"It has its good points," she said. "A few bad ones, too."

"I'm not sure of the company."

The lines in his face were deeper than the last time she'd seen him, nearly six years ago. She wondered if hers were as well.

"I've worked with Glass," she said. "He's solid. If it wasn't for him, I wouldn't be here."

"It's his cousin I'm worried about. He's in over his head."

"I know," she said. They'd left the airport, were on a long stretch of elevated highway. In the distance, she could see the lights of the city.

"I've never been much for taking off dealers," he said. "Too unpredictable, too much risk."

"Usually, yeah."

"On the other hand, aren't many places to find cash these days. At least not in any amount worth taking. Dealers are always a standby in that respect. That's one economy that never slumps."

She opened the glove box, took out the pink rental contract. She saw he'd rented the car at the airport the day before, in the name Louis Brown.

"Sticking with the LB," she said.

"Makes it easier. You worried this was a government car? Wired up?"

"Like you said, just being careful. No offense."

"None taken."

She put the contract back in the glove box, closed it.

"Way I see it," he said, "this Cordell's taking a hell of a risk."

"He must think it's worth it."

"You believe there's that much money involved? Half a million?"

"Could be. Even if it's half that, though, not a bad day's work for four people."

They rode in silence for a while, the freeway taking them over an area of dark factories and warehouses, dimly lit streets that seemed to go on forever.

"This town's seen better days," she said.

"So have I."

"You still in St. Louis?"

"Off and on. Was down in Florida for a while. Got a wife there. Well, ex-wife now. Little girl, too."

"How old?"

"Six. Her name's Haley. I know, hard to believe, right? A kid at my age. Didn't plan it that way, just sort of happened."

"Nothing wrong with that. Congratulations."

"Thanks. Things didn't quite work out the way I hoped, though."

"You see her?"

"Haley? Not much. They're down near Orlando. I bought a house for them, send money when I can."

She thought of Maddie, her own daughter. Eleven this year, and being raised by Crissa's cousin in Texas, with no idea who her real mother was. Crissa sent them money every month, certified checks from a Costa Rican account.

"I heard about Wayne," he said. "About his sentence being extended. I'm sorry."

"Thanks."

"That's a tough break."

"It was. His parole hearing was coming up. I almost had him out of there."

It was Wayne who'd brought her into the Life. Before that had been a series of bad relationships marked by casual violence and petty crime. She'd been with Beaumont, Maddie's father, for only a year, blurred months of drugs and alcohol.

Wayne had taken her away from all that. He lived well, showed her a life she never thought possible. He put crews together, did work all over the country. Eighteen years younger than him, but she'd become part of that world as well.

"You ever get down there to see him?" Larry said.

"I did for a while, regular. But the name they had on file down there on the approved visitors roll, the one I was using . . . I had to give that up, because of some things that happened. They had my picture, too. I can't go back."

"That's rough. I'm sorry."

"Nothing for it," she said. "Just the way it played out."

"I still feel responsible for what happened. In Texas."

"You weren't."

She and Wayne were living in Delaware when it all went wrong. Weak with the flu, she'd stayed behind when Wayne, Larry, and another man took down a jewelry wholesaler outside Houston. It was supposed to be a give-up by the owner, but a clerk had pulled a gun, shot Wayne in the shoulder. Larry had carried him out of there, but two blocks later, their driver put the car into a fire hydrant and park bench. Larry got away before the police arrived, but Wayne and the driver drew bids for armed robbery and conspiracy, ten to fifteen each.

"I maybe could have gotten him out of that car," Larry said. "But the shape he was in, he wouldn't have made it very far."

"I know."

"I had a cracked collarbone myself. Spent the night in the crawl space under a broken-down porch 'bout a block away, listening to sirens and radios all night. I was so fucked up, I couldn't tell when I was awake and when I was dreaming. Next morning, I could hardly move. Never did heal right."

"You did what you could," she said. "You got him out of that store, gave him a chance. You didn't leave him there."

"Couldn't, after all he'd done for me. He brought me in on plenty of work, set me up with a stake when I needed it. I owe him."

"We all do."

They exited the freeway, turned down a wide residential street. Big stone houses, fenced-in yards. But after a while, fewer houses were lit, and the streetlights were dark. Overgrown yards now, boarded-up windows. He touched the button to lock the doors.

"Sure you know where you're going?" she said.

"I was here yesterday. I think I got it."

They steered around a shopping cart on its side in the middle of the street. He made a right, then a left, and they were on a block lit by a single streetlamp halfway down.

The house was near the end of the block. He turned into the driveway, their headlights passing across plywooded front windows. It was a two-story house, gray stone, a rich man's home long ago. A bay window faced the driveway, most of its glass intact. Beneath it was a tangle of weeds and shrubbery.

There was a garage in the rear, a silver Lexus parked beside it. He K-turned, backed in alongside the Lexus.

"You carrying?" she said.

He shook his head, looked at the house, the car ticking and cooling. The rear windows were boarded over, gang tags sprayed across the plywood, but the back door was ajar, darkness inside.

"Didn't think I'd need it," he said. "I flew here anyway, couldn't bring anything. And there was no time to find something after I got to town. You?"

"No. Same reason." She thought of the Glock 9 she kept in a safe at home, the smaller .32 Beretta Tomcat clipped to the springs under her bed. Wished she had one of them now.

"Nervous?" he said.

"A little."

"You vouched for Glass, said he's solid."

"I did. And he is. Or at least he was, last time we did work together."

"Still, no way to be sure what we're walking into here, is there?"

They looked at the house, neither of them moving.

"Only one way to find out," she said, and opened the door.

THREE

Cordell and Glass were in the big living room, a map open on the coffee table between them, bottles of Heineken beside it. The room was lit by two Coleman battery lanterns a few feet apart.

"Hey," Glass said. "Come on in."

He sat on a ragged couch, Cordell in a chair across from him. The hardwood floor was littered with trash. Chunks of plaster had fallen from the ceiling, lathe showing through. A bricked-in fireplace in one wall, a wide staircase that went up into darkness.

"I know," Glass said. "Sorry. Best we could do on short notice."

"You ought to put something over that window," she said. "The light."

"Doesn't matter," Cordell said. "No one around here to see it."

A plastic vial crunched under her boot heel. She swept it away with her foot. "Whose place is this?"

"No one's now," Glass said. "Cordell found it. This block, you can take your pick. Plenty to choose from."

"No one's been here in a long time," Cordell said. "No neighbors, either. Every house on the block about the same as this. Mayor's been trying to get people to relocate closer to the city center, so they cut off services to some of these outer neighborhoods. Didn't take people long to get the message."

Larry had moved to her right. Without a word, he'd taken the lead when they'd entered the house.

"We're going over some street routes," Glass said. "Can't be sure on the drop-off point until we get word, but it'll likely be in the same general area."

"Unless Marquis changes up," she said.

"He won't," Cordell said. "He'll stick to somewhere he knows, and he don't know anything but downtown. He's the king there, that's the way he thinks. That's his kingdom. No one will mess with him there."

There were two metal folding chairs leaning against a wall. Larry opened them, dusted off the seats, set them near the table. A moth fluttered around one of the lanterns.

"More beers out in the kitchen," Glass said. "If you want one."

"Sounds good," Larry said, and went back out. He'd take his time, she knew, look around. She sat. Glass pulled a lantern closer, then turned the map around so she could read it. There were three routes traced on it, one in blue, one red, and one yellow.

When she looked up, Cordell was watching her.

"Problem?" she said.

"Just surprised is all. When my cuz said he could bring some people in, I didn't expect a woman."

"Got an issue with that?"

"Not at all. Like I said, just surprised. But it's all good."

Larry came back in with two Heinekens. He put one on the table in front of her, then turned the other chair around, straddled it. He set his beer on the floor.

"We need to take these bottles with us when we go," she said. "And you-all need to wipe down anything around here you may have touched." She was the only one wearing gloves.

"We will," Glass said.

She picked up the bottle, took a sip. It was lukewarm. She rarely drank beer, but better to go along with everyone now, keep them comfortable.

Larry pointed at the map. "If the drop-off's near where it was today, how long to get out of the city, back here?"

"That's what I was just working out," Glass said. "Couple ways to go. Way I see it, we keep a transfer car close to the drop site, wherever that turns out to be, then switch over. We'll be out of the city itself in fifteen minutes, maybe a little more. Then we meet back here, do the cut."

"So we need two vehicles," Larry said.

"That's right. The jump-out car, then the transfer."

"Three," she said.

Glass looked at her.

"We don't want that Armada chasing after us," she said. "We need to block it off, disable it. Someone has to do that the same time we're pulling the money out of that car. So we need two vehicles going in. Probably a good idea to have two transfers afterward as well, so we can split up faster, head back here."

"So four cars altogether," Glass said.

"Better a van for the jump-out," she said. "Delivery van, bread truck, something like that. Easy to get in and out of. Back doors stay open, engine running. We pop that trunk, get the bag, everyone gets inside the van quick. Otherwise, with a car, even a four-door, we're doing a Chinese fire drill, everybody tripping over each other getting in and out."

"Makes sense," Glass said.

To Cordell, she said, "How do they keep the money? How's it packed?"

"Duffel bag. Big one. Kind people carry sports equipment in, hockey sticks and shit."

"Is the money banded?"

"Yeah. Marquis, Damien, and the boy Metro do the counting themselves. Don't trust anyone else. Marquis's got an office above the garage he runs, that's where he does his business. They've got a safe there, counting machines, everything he needs. Nobody gets in or out while it's going on."

"Maybe we should hit the office instead," Larry said. "Bound to be more money in the safe than what they're dropping off."

Cordell shook his head. "He's got an army up in there.

Surveillance cameras, too. No one can get up those stairs without him knowing it. Steel door. All he has to do is lock it, wait for whoever's outside to go away. If they even get that far."

"The drop-off's the vulnerable point," Glass said. "Rip and run. One of us drives. Two of us hit the car, get the trunk open and the bag out. Another one faces off those boys in the Armada, like you said, keeps them occupied. Then we load up and we're gone."

"Cordell should drive the van," she said. "We don't want him out on the street. Even with a mask, someone might recognize him, hear his voice. He should stay up front."

Glass looked at him. "You okay with that?"

"Driving? Yeah, I guess."

"Better for everyone if you're behind the wheel," she said. "Off the street."

"Whatever."

"What about the second vehicle?" Glass said.

"We'll leave it behind. We won't need it anymore." She took a slip of paper from her jacket pocket. On it was a list she'd written back at the hotel. She handed it to Glass.

"What I think we'll need," she said. "As we work it out, there might be more. But this is a start. We should get on these as soon as we can."

He looked at the list. "Smoke grenades?"

"If you can find them. If not, we'll have to figure something else out."

"How about tear gas instead?" Larry said.

"Problem is the wind," she said. "A shift in direction, and it'll blow back on us. That means we'll need gas masks as well, another complication. Smoke will do. It'll give us the time we need."

"And the Armada?" Glass said. "What about that?"

"I have some ideas." She took another sip of beer, looked at Cordell. "Who else knows about this?"

"What?"

"Who did you tell? Girlfriend? Wife?"

He seemed confused for a moment: "Nobody."

"Who's Marquis going to come looking for if he can't find you? Family, friends? You'll be putting them in danger, too, afterward."

"No one."

"You sure on that?"

"I haven't told anyone shit about this."

"Marquis won't know that," she said. "He'll ask around, right? He'll ask hard."

"It's cool. No worries there."

She looked at Glass. He shrugged.

"Okay, then," she said. "Let's take another look at that map."

An hour later, driving back to her hotel, Larry said, "Feel better?"

"A little."

"It sounds good to me," he said. "At least, what I've heard. Not much exposure. Done and gone, especially the way you laid it out."

"It has its issues."

"They all do. What part's bothering you?"

"Cordell. He knows a lot. The money, the drop-offs, the time and locations. When he vanishes, Marquis will take it for granted he's involved."

"That's the risk."

"Say he doesn't get away in time, or he goes somewhere stupid and obvious. Marquis catches up with him, he leads them right to us, or at least to Charlie."

"I was thinking the same," he said. "But there's not much we can do about it."

They were back on the elevated freeway now, dark streets below them.

"Almost forgot to tell you," he said. "Bobby Chance says hello."

She looked at him. "You talked to him?"

"I was out his way a few months back, looking at some work. Tracked him down to see if he was interested, but he said he's out of the Game now. Whole thing fell through anyway."

"Where is he?"

"Lives on a farm in southern Ohio. Got a woman with him. Might be his wife for all I know."

"How's he doing?"

"Shoulder's still screwed up, from that buckshot he caught. He told me what happened."

The last time she'd seen Chance had been outside a Connecticut emergency room. She'd left him there, gunshot and semiconscious, after some work they'd done together had gone bad. They'd taken down a high-stakes poker game in Florida, and a man had come looking for them, trying to recover the money. It had all ended in Connecticut. They'd left a dead body and a burning house behind them.

"That was a bad time," she said.

"He's on the straight now, or so he says. They've got a working soybean field there they rent out. Outside of that, though, I don't see he's doing much of anything."

"He still use Sladden?" That was Chance's contact in Kansas City, his go-between.

"Far as I know. That's how I found him."

"I'll have to look him up someday."

"He'd like that. He says you saved his life."

"I'm the one got him into all that trouble in the first place."

"Not the way he tells it."

They saw the first signs for the airport.

"Here's what I'm thinking," she said. "We stick it out here, organize as much as we can. We've got at least a week until the next drop. If something doesn't feel right between now and then, we cut our losses, go our separate ways."

"Makes sense. But . . ."

"What?"

"Work like this, sometimes, even if everything doesn't line up the way you want, it's worth the risk. Because of the payoff."

"You're taking their word for how much money's in there."

"If this guy—Marquis or whatever his name is—is moving that much product on a regular basis, five hundred K is nothing," he said. "These inner-city dope slingers bring in so much money, they don't know what to do with it. That's what always gets them in trouble, the money."

"And the bodies."

"That, too."

"You know how they catch monkeys in the Pacific?" she said.

He looked at her. "What?"

"Monkeys. In the jungle. Somebody told me this story once. They're hard to catch because they're so fast, climbing trees, jumping from branch to branch. Good eating, but you can't get near them."

"I'm not following you."

"What the natives do is hollow out a coconut, leave just the right size hole, put a nut or some fruit inside. Monkey sees it, can't resist. He reaches in, grabs the fruit, but when he makes a fist, he can't get his hand back out. That's the way the natives find them, coconut hanging from their arm. Can't climb a tree, can't do much of anything one-handed. Then they kill them and eat them."

"What's your point?"

"The monkey dies because it can't let go of what it's after, even if it knows it's gonna be caught."

"Okay," he said. "I get it. Don't be a monkey."

"Something like that."

"Here's another way to look at it. We do the work and haul ass, get as far away as we can, let cousin Cordell catch the fallout. He doesn't know anything about us anyway, does he?"

"Charlie would tell him only what he needed to know."

"You say Glass is a pro."

"He is."

"Then he'll know when to cut his losses, too. His cousin

is an amateur. He's aware of that already. He's probably thinking the same thing we are."

"Maybe," she said. "But at the moment, Cordell's in it with us. He's working the setup, running the risks. If that changes, it changes. But right now, he's one of us. We have to respect that. If not, why go in with him in the first place?"

"That sounds like Wayne talking."

"You don't agree?"

"I guess I do, right now. Later might be an issue. And there is one way to make sure."

"What's that?"

"We do the work, then pop Cordell. End of story."

"Not an option."

"You say that now."

"Well, then," she said. "Let's hope it doesn't come to that."

FOUR

She was at the window of her hotel room, watching a plane climb into the overcast, when her cell phone buzzed. It was a gray afternoon and a light rain was falling, drops speckling the glass.

"It's Sunday," Charlie Glass said. The phone was a disposable she'd bought two days ago. Only he and Larry had the number.

Four days since the meeting at the house. She'd spent it going to movies, restaurants, or sitting in the room, working the whole thing through in her head. Long ago, she'd learned to wait, let things play out, then step in, make her move when the time was right. But now she was restless, eager to do the work. Eager to get home after it was done.

"Three days," she said. "That doesn't give us much time."

"I've been working on that list. I've got almost everything you wanted, what we talked about."

"That was fast."

"I had some of it already, things I knew we'd need. We can go over it all when we meet."

"Your cousin sure on the day?"

"Sure as he can be under the circumstances. He got the word same way he always does."

"Location?"

"He'll know that tomorrow."

"How's he doing?"

"What do you mean?"

"I'm wondering if he's cut out for this." She watched a second plane follow the track of the first one, disappear into the low clouds.

"He's committed, if that's what you're asking. He knows what he's getting into."

"Does he?"

"He isn't like us. This is a one-off for him. He saw an opportunity, that's all. I'm schooling him best I can. He'll be all right."

"He understand from here out, everything's different? There's no going back?"

"He does."

"He's your responsibility."

"I know that."

"Good," she said. "When do you want to meet?"

"Seven. That work for you? We've got a lot to go over."

"I'll call our mutual friend. What about the vehicle we discussed?"

"Got it today. You can look it over when you get here."

"You're putting up a lot."

"Just an investment."

"Let's hope it pays off."

"I'm betting it will. See you tonight."

In the car, Larry said, "Under the seat."

She reached down, felt only carpet, springs.

"Toward the back."

She bent, reached until her fingers closed on a plastic bag. She drew it out, opened it, looked at the pistol inside. It was a Mini Glock 9 mm, black plastic and metal, with a square trigger guard.

"Where'd you get this?" she said.

"Made some calls. Easy thing to do in this town, buy a gun."

"Is it clean?" She turned it over in her hand, ejected the magazine, saw the brass cartridges inside.

"So I was told. We'll dump it afterward anyway, first chance we get."

"Does it work?"

"I test-fired it," he said. "It's good."

She slid the magazine back into the grip until it seated. "Get one yourself?"

"Better safe." He touched his waist beneath the jacket.

They were on the edge of the city now, passing industrial

buildings with broken windows, grassy parking lots. She slipped the Glock under her jacket, wedged it into the belt at the small of her back. It felt right.

They drove in silence the rest of the way. When they reached the block of empty houses, he slowed, watching the rearview for headlights, someone following them. But the street was clear as far back as they could see. He turned into the driveway.

There was another vehicle parked near the Lexus now, a gray tarp spread across it, only the tires visible.

"There's your van," he said.

He parked alongside. They got out, and she took the penlight from her jacket pocket, thumbed it on. She lifted an edge of the tarp. Beneath was a white service van. A magnetic sign on the driver's door read EAST SIDE PLUMBING.

She raised the tarp. Dents and body rust, but the tires were good.

"What do you think?" he said.

"Looks good enough. Let's hope it runs."

They went into the house. Cordell and Glass were in the living room, Cordell leaning against a wall. Glass was in one of the folding chairs, map spread out on the table, a lantern pulled close. No beer this time. Laid out on the couch were four dark-blue Kevlar vests with Velcro straps. On the floor was a black tactical bag, unzipped far enough to show the glint of dark metal inside.

Glass looked up as they came in.

"You look happy," she said.

"I am." He touched a red X on the map. "Cordell came through. We've got it."

She looked at Cordell. He nodded to her.

"Good to hear," Larry said.

"There's a problem, though," Glass said. "Change of plans."

"What?" she said.

"Different time frame."

"What's that mean?"

"They changed up on the drop-off," Cordell said. "They do that sometimes, at the last minute. I just found out 'bout an hour ago."

"It's sooner than we thought," Glass said.

She looked at him. "How soon?"

"Tomorrow."

"Not enough time."

"If you want to walk," Glass said, "I understand. But I think we can do this."

She looked at Larry. He shook his head. She turned back to Glass. "No good."

"It's not what we thought we'd have," he said. "But it can still work. Hear me out at least. We've got everything we need. We just have to move up the timetable a little."

"He's right," Cordell said. "Everything else still the same. I'm hearing five hundred and fifty K this time. Straight up."

She looked at Larry again. He shrugged.

After a moment, she took the other folding chair, dragged it toward the table.

"You've got five minutes," she said. "Convince me."

* * *

They were in a suburb north of the city, parked on a residential street, lights and engine off. Almost midnight, and both of them cold. Larry had run the engine for a while for heat, but she worried the exhaust would show in the chill air, draw attention to them, so he'd shut it off. They'd been here almost two hours now.

"Times like this, I wish I still smoked," he said. "Something to do with my hands at least."

A half block ahead, a dark red Chevy Silverado 4x4 pickup was parked in the driveway of a two-story house. It was a middle-class neighborhood. Well-kept yards, garages. A world away from the place Cordell had found.

After they'd left the house, they'd driven up to the suburbs, scouted restaurant and movie theater lots until they found what she was looking for, a big pickup with a heavy-duty pushbar. They'd sat on it for an hour, until a crowd had come out of the theater, and a man and woman had driven away in the truck. They'd followed it here, had been watching ever since. A half hour ago, the first-floor lights in the house had gone out, leaving two lit windows above. A square of light fell across the Silverado's roof.

"What if there's an alarm?" he said.

"Have to take my chances with that. Try to override it quick as I can."

"Don't spend too much time on it. If those downstairs lights go on again, come back quick. We'll find another rig somewhere else."

"We're running out of time. I don't want to have to start looking again."

She shifted in her seat, the Glock cold against her back.

"So you're good with all this," he said. "I'm surprised."

"Charlie's right. The basic plan's still solid. Another day to prep would be better, but you play the hand you're dealt."

"What about Wayne's Five P's? 'Proper Planning . . .'"

"'Prevents Poor Performance.' You've got a good memory."

"Hard to forget that one."

"He was right. But this time I don't think we have the luxury."

One of the upstairs lights went out. She reached beneath the seat, took out the chamois bag Glass had given her, loosened the drawstring. Inside was a hinged metal slim jim, a flathead screwdriver, vise grips, and four lengths of wire with alligator clips at each end.

"I used to know how to do that back in the day," he said. "But these new cars, forget about it. I wouldn't know where to start."

"Same principles."

"Maybe. But I'm an old horse. I can't work smarter, I can only work harder."

"Not so old. You got some years left."

She took the Glock from her belt, bent and slid it under the seat. If she was stopped in the Silverado, she didn't want it on her.

The last window went dark. The only illumination now was a streetlight a half block up.

"How long should we give it?" he said.

She inched a glove back to look at her watch. "Half hour,

at least. Let them get to sleep. We'll see if any of those lights go back on."

She flexed her fingers. It had been a long time since she'd stolen a vehicle. If she screwed it up, got caught, it would all be over, the whole thing ended before it had begun.

She went through the contents of the bag, getting the feel of the tools so she could work smoothly once inside the Silverado, not waste any time.

"Lately I've been thinking about this life," he said. "Choices I made. Things I gave up. Wondering if it was all worth it."

"You could always get a job."

"That ship sailed a long time ago."

"Then you don't have much choice, do you?"

"I don't know. Lately it seems the work's getting harder and the money's getting smaller. It's like they say, you can make a killing in this business, but you can't make a living."

When the half hour was up, she said, "See you back at the house," and opened the door.

She crossed the street, bag under her arm, fighting the urge to walk faster. Up the driveway now, the point of no return. She looked up at the dark second floor, then took out the slim jim, unfolded it.

As she'd expected, the driver's door was locked. The slim jim slid easily between the weather-stripping and the window.

She found the locking rod on the first sweep, pulled up, and the door opened. A red light blinked on the dash. She climbed up into the seat, went to work with the screwdriver, got the plastic panel off the steering column just as the alarm began to bleat. It was clumsy work with the gloves, but she found the right wires, used the alligator clips. The alarm went silent.

There was no keyguard on the ignition, so she didn't need the vise grips. The screwdriver was enough. She forced it into the ignition slot, twisted. Something cracked inside the steering column, and the engine came to life. She looked up at the windows. Still dark.

She backed down the driveway, bumped into the street, straightened out, gave it gas. Larry started his engine, pulled out behind her, keeping his distance. If she got stopped, she'd ditch the truck, make a run for it, and he'd come back later, try to find her. It wasn't much of a plan, but it was all they had.

At the next block, she turned on the headlights. The engine was running smoothly. She came to a red light, switched on her blinker, waited. She looked in the rearview, expecting to see flashing lights, police cruisers. All she saw was Larry's rental, coming to a stop behind her.

When the light changed, she let out her breath, made the turn. A block later, when the trembling in her hands had stopped, she turned on the radio. Soft jazz came from the speakers. She followed the signs for Route 75, headed south. They'd stow the truck in the garage tonight, make their final preparations. A few hours to sleep, and then the work. And by this time tomorrow night, all of it over. One way or another.

FIVE

She was up at dawn, watery light coming through the gap in the curtains. It had been a thin sleep, and she'd woken a half-dozen times during the night. It felt better to be up and moving, getting ready.

The tension was already in her stomach, and she knew she wouldn't be able to eat. She showered and dressed, then used the coffeemaker in the bathroom to brew a cup, dosed it with three packets of sugar. She carried it to the window, opened the curtains. It was raining again, streaking the glass. They'd have to factor that in.

She packed her things, then checked the Mini Glock, wrapped two thick rubber bands around its grip. They would keep it from slipping in her hand, or sliding down too far in her beltline. Before she left Detroit, she'd disassemble the gun, scatter the parts. It was too risky to travel with it. She'd take a late-night bus to Toledo, then catch an Amtrak train to Buffalo. From there, she'd rent a car, drive the eight hours back to New Jersey.

She was back at the window, looking out at the rain and sipping her second cup of coffee, when the cell phone on the nightstand began to buzz. She looked at it. Larry's number. It sounded twice, then stopped. It was their signal. He was waiting for her in the lot, ready to go.

She tucked the Glock into the small of her back, pulled on her leather jacket. At the door, she took one last look at the room, wondering if she'd forgotten anything. Her suitcase was packed and ready, standing beside the bed. That and the rumpled sheets were the only signs anyone had been here at all.

They suited up in the living room, the lanterns on. The house was cold, with a dampness she felt in her joints. There was a slow, steady drip from the kitchen ceiling, a puddle on the linoleum floor.

She strapped the Kevlar vest on over her T-shirt, tightened the Velcro, then pulled on the black sweater and dark windbreaker. She'd left her leather in Larry Black's trunk.

She checked her watch: 12:45. The drop-off was scheduled for 2:00, but they didn't know how much time they had before the pickup. They'd have to move fast.

Charlie Glass handed out cell phones and earpieces. "Numbers are already programmed in, One through Four. Just in case we get separated. I'm One." He pointed at Cordell.

"You're Two." Then at Crissa, and finally Larry. "Three and Four."

"Got it," she said.

Cordell was struggling with his vest. It hung crooked on his back, the straps uneven.

"Hold on," she said, and came up behind him. She pulled the Velcro loose to free the right-hand strap, adjusted it until the vest was tight.

"Thanks," he said. His face was shiny with sweat.

"You okay?"

"Little nervous, I guess. Ain't no thing."

"It's normal. It'll pass."

She'd seen it before, with veterans as well as first-timers. Jumpy at first, then calmer as things got going. Once there was a task at hand, things to do, a timetable, it was better. But now, before it started, there was time to think, and that was never good.

"You set with directions to the transfers?" Glass said to him. "I don't want you out there driving around, 'Left? Right? Where the fuck am I?'"

"I got it," Cordell said.

"You'll be fine," she said. "In a couple hours we'll all be back here. It'll be done."

The black tactical bag Glass had brought for her was on the couch. She unzipped it, looked inside: two olive-drab M 18 smoke grenades with red tops, a pistol-grip Mossberg shotgun with shoulder strap, two boxes of shells, a street map, a ski mask, and a plastic mouthguard still in its package. She took out the Mossberg, worked the pump to check the action. It cycled smoothly, and the strap would make it easier to handle on the street.

She opened the boxes of shells, spilled them onto the table—double-O buck and three-inch deer slugs. Bracing the Mossberg's butt on her hip, she thumbed shells into the loading port until she felt the pressure of the spring.

"What you wanted?" Glass said. He had his own windbreaker on, was loading a blued revolver.

"It'll work," she said. She pumped to chamber a shell, then fed a fresh one into the port. The extra rounds went into her jacket pockets. "Still like those wheel guns, huh?"

"They don't jam. And no brass to pick up, if you have to use it."

She put on the safety, slid the shotgun back in the bag.

"You'll be there first," he said. "As soon as you're in place, hit me on the cell."

"Right." They'd been through it all already. She activated her phone, checked the speed dial, saw the numbers he'd programmed. She put the phone and earpiece in the tac bag.

Cordell was sitting on one of the folding chairs, looking at the floor. He was breathing fast. She looked at Glass. He'd seen it, too.

"He going to make it?" Larry said. He was assembling an AR-15 rifle, fitting the parts into place.

Cordell raised his head. He looked sick. "I'll be all right."

"You better be," Glass said. "Time to man up, brother. Everybody waiting on you."

"Deep breaths," she said. "In through the nose, out through the mouth. Slow."

He braced his hands on his knees, drew in air.

"Slow," she said again.

He nodded. "I'm good."

"You will be," she said. "All you have to do is drive. We've got everything else. It'll all be over before you know it."

"We need to get going," Larry said.

She zipped the tac bag shut, slung the strap over her left shoulder. "Better give me ten minutes. We don't want a convoy leaving here. If there's a problem . . ." She nodded at Cordell's back. "Let me know."

"Won't be any problem," Glass said.

"Then I'll see you there," she said.

It was a VW Jetta this time, at least ten years old, parked on a one-way street in a block of warehouses. The Armada was already in place, a block behind on the opposite side. Wipers thumping, she drove past, knew the men inside would be watching her. Passing the Jetta, she saw the Tigers cap on the back deck.

No other vehicles around. The warehouse windows were dark. Two blocks up, she made a left. Shuttered businesses lined both sides of the street here, auto body shops, tire stores. She went another block and pulled into a service alley, out of sight from the street.

The clouds were lower now, the rain steady. She pulled the

tac bag up onto the console, got out the phone, fit in the earpiece, pressed 1.

When Glass answered, she said, "I'm here. It's right where it's supposed to be. Blue VW, Michigan plates."

"Good. The Armada?"

"Same setup as last time. One-way street. They're a block down on the left-hand side."

"Anyone else around?"

"Not that I've seen."

"We're parked about a mile away, ready to roll."

"Call when you're close."

She hit END, took a breath. The Silverado chugged around her. She'd left the engine on, didn't want to risk a problem starting it again, fumbling with wires. Beneath the vest, her T-shirt was damp with sweat.

She watched the alley entrance in the rearview. It was unlikely the men in the Armada would get suspicious, follow her, leave the Jetta unattended. But if they did, she didn't want to be boxed in.

She took the Glock from her belt, ejected the magazine, pushed down on the shells to test the spring pressure. Then she palmed the magazine home again, heard it click. She eased back the slide to check the round in the chamber.

The phone buzzed. Glass.

"Three blocks away," he said. "We're stopped. Waiting on you."

"Going now."

The phone and earpiece went back into the tac bag, the Glock into her belt. She took a deep breath, held it in, felt the tightness in her stomach. All the planning, the waiting, had led to this.

She reversed down the alley, out onto the empty street, swung the Silverado around to face the way she'd come. She waited there, watching the intersection two blocks ahead, half-expecting the Armada to come after her. For the second driver to appear. For the whole thing to fall apart.

She opened the package, fit the mouthguard over her teeth and bit down. It tasted like rubber. She pulled on the ski mask, adjusted the eyeholes, checked the seat belt and shoulder harness to make sure they were tight.

Ahead of her, the blacktop glistened. Two blocks and a right turn. They wouldn't expect a vehicle to come at them like that, down a one-way in the wrong direction. It might cut into their reaction time, give her the edge she needed. But she'd have to be careful on the wet road, not lose control when she made the turn, go into a skid.

She clamped down on the mouthguard, gave the Silverado gas. It surged forward, gaining speed, and then the intersection was looming up, the STOP and NO RIGHT TURN signs. She worked the brake and gas, the truck fishtailing as it swung around the corner, tires squealing.

Watch your speed, she thought. Watch the road. She passed the Jetta, headed toward the Armada, saw the white van beyond it, coming in her direction, still a block away. She twisted the wheel, lined up the Silverado's pushbar with the Armada's grille. At the last moment, she took her foot off the gas, floored the brake.

The Silverado was still doing thirty, tires screeching, when its pushbar smashed into the Armada's front end. The impact drove the Armada back, flung her forward against the harness, and then the air bag detonated, filling the space in front of her, pushing her back into the seat.

Quiet then, except for the sound of the wipers. She sat stunned for a moment, the deflated air bag in her lap, white powder everywhere, a smell like gunsmoke in the air. The Armada was half up on the sidewalk, windshield cracked, steam billowing from beneath the buckled hood. The Silverado's pushbar was buried deep in its grille.

She shifted into reverse, touched the gas, and the truck pulled away. Pieces of the Armada's grille clattered into the street. She put the shifter in park, unsnapped the seat belt, pulled the Mossberg from the tac bag and thumbed off the safety. The van passed her without slowing.

No movement in the Armada. She opened her door, got down fast, circling to her left in the rain, the shotgun coming up. She fired into the Armada's right front tire, the rubber exploding, stray buckshot pocking the fender. She worked the pump, a smoking shell flying free, then fired at the left front, shredded it. The front end of the Armada sank like a tired horse.

The next two rounds were deer slugs. She pumped, fired into what was left of the grille, pumped and fired again, heard the heavy rounds punch through into the engine. More steam hissed out, green coolant spilling onto the blacktop. She fired over the roof then, a warning to anyone inside to stay down.

No time to pick up casings. She slung the shotgun over

her left shoulder, moved back behind the cover of the open door, took a smoke grenade from the bag. She pulled the pin, popped the spoon, and rolled the canister beneath the Armada. Thick pinkish-red smoke began to hiss out. The second grenade came up against the flat right front tire, smoke billowing up. In seconds, the Armada was almost hidden.

The Mossberg went back into the tac bag, the bag's carry strap over her shoulder. She ran back toward the Jetta. The van was alongside it, back doors open. Glass and Larry, both in ski masks, were at the Jetta's trunk, working a prybar into the lock mechanism.

She rolled up her mask, took out the mouthguard, and dropped it in the tac bag. She reached the Jetta just as the trunk popped open. Larry looked inside and said, "Son of a bitch."

She came up beside them. There was nothing in the trunk but a worn tire, a pair of jumper cables, and a green army blanket.

"Goddammit," Glass said, and then she bent, hooked gloved fingers around the inner rim of the tire, dragged it out onto the street, let it wobble and fall. "Underneath," she said.

Glass pulled the blanket away, and there in the wheel well was a dark blue duffel bag. Larry caught a strap, dragged the bag out of the trunk. It thudded on the ground.

"Hurry," she said, and looked back at the Armada. The smoke was clearing, the rain keeping it down, the Armada smeared red from it. She heard metal squeal, someone trying to open a door from inside. It was bent, wedged shut by the impact.

Glass took the other end of the duffel, and he and Larry carried it to the van, swung it inside and followed it in. Crissa handed the tac bag to Glass, scrambled up after them, heard a metallic clack behind her, and then something punched her hard in the back, sent her forward. Her legs went out from under her, and she hit the bumper going down, landed on her side on the wet blacktop. The echo of the shot rolled down the street.

You're hit, she thought, and twisted to look behind her, saw a black man standing beside the Armada in the rain, a rifle at his shoulder. There's that AK Cordell told us about, she thought. Then the rifle cracked again, and a divot blew out of the blacktop near her face, sprayed her with grit.

She rolled to the right, and there was the sound of another shot above her. She looked up, saw Larry Black on one knee in the door of the van, the AR-15 at his shoulder, calmly taking aim again.

He and the black man fired almost simultaneously. The van's left back window exploded, cubes of safety glass raining down on her. She looked back, saw the man with the AK stumbling, trying to bring the gun up again. Larry fired above her again, a flat crack, and the man spun and went down.

There were hands on her now, dragging her up into the van. She saw the gray sky above her, and then she was in, facedown across the duffel, the van pulling away, both doors still open. Glass fell across her, and Larry caught the collar of his jacket, pulled him away from the open doors. The van swayed as it took the corner, spilling them to the side. Larry dropped the AR-15, put a hand against the wall to brace himself. They turned another corner, tires squealing, one of the doors swinging shut.

"Slow down!" Glass yelled. The noise of the engine changed, and the van stopped swaying. Glass got to his feet, pulled the other door shut until it latched.

Larry knelt beside her. "You hit?"

She nodded, couldn't catch her breath to speak. Her back was numb. He pulled off her ski mask, said, "Help me turn her over," and he and Glass rolled her gently onto her side. She went with it, feeling the first stabs of pain then. They got the windbreaker off her, and then Larry had a knife out, was cutting at her sweater. It came away in two parts. He took the Glock from her belt, pulled at the Velcro straps of the vest. She heard the crackle as they were undone, and then a weight seemed to lift off her.

"Vest stopped it," he said. "Barely."

The numbness was fading, replaced by a burning knot of pain under her right shoulder blade. It brought water to her eyes. Pain is good, she thought. Movement is good. You've been shot in the back. You should be dead or paralyzed, and you're neither.

Glass tugged off his ski mask, his face slick with sweat. "Just the one?"

"I think so," she said. She took a breath. "First time I've ever been shot."

"If you're lucky," Larry said, "it'll be the last."

She could feel the duffel under her, the edge of something

hard. Larry took off his mask, sat beside her. Glass slumped against the wall, sank down. Wind whistled through the shattered window.

She rolled onto her knees, pulled the duffel to her, unzipped it. Banded packs of money inside, the bag almost full. She reached under them, began to root around.

"What are you looking for?" Glass said.

Her hand met something rigid and cold. She took it out. A black box the size of a cigarette pack, a single green light blinking on one side.

"This."

"GPS," Larry said. "Goddammit. We should have known."

"Toss it," she said.

"I'll do better than that," Glass said. He took it from her, got up, dropped it on the floor, put one hand on the wall for balance, and brought his boot heel down hard. They heard plastic crack, then splinter the second time the boot came down. When he took his foot away, the light was out, the transponder in three pieces. He picked them up, fed them out through the broken window.

She crawled until her back was against the wall. Hooking a heel in the vest, she dragged it closer, turned it over. She could see the indentation where the round had struck. She rubbed a gloved thumb across it. At closer range, the bullet would have gone straight through.

"Told you it was a good idea," Larry said.

She looked at him, and he was grinning. She felt the tension break inside her for the first time that day. "Yeah," she said. "I guess it was."

Then she was laughing, her eyes watering, the stress and fear and pain all coming out at once, the knowledge of what they had done, what she had survived. Larry was laughing now, too. Charlie Glass sat against the opposite wall, watching them.

"Y'all are crazy," he said, and looked away, but he couldn't hide his grin.

SIX

The van slowed, came to a stop. Charlie Glass looked through the shattered window. "It's clear."

The engine cut off, and he opened the doors. They were in the rear playground of a school, the windows plywooded over, graffiti scrawled on the stone walls. The transfer cars—a green Saturn and a blue Toyota—were parked beside a chain-link fence. They'd been stolen the day before, left there that morning. They were both a few years old, innocuous.

Glass jumped down. "Let's move."

Larry stood, helped her to her feet. She winced as a spasm of pain tightened her back. Glass reached up to her, but she waved him away, climbed down, legs unsteady. She picked up the Glock, stuck it in her belt, then got the windbreaker from the floor, turned it right side out, saw the bullet hole.

Larry had disassembled the AR-15, put the parts in the

tac bag along with the shotgun and Glass's revolver. He gestured to the Glock. She shook her head.

"Everything's going in the river," he said. "You know that."

"Yeah, but until then, I'll feel better with it on me." She pulled on the jacket.

"Suit yourself," he said. He zipped the tac bag shut, climbed down. "You all right?"

"I will be." Her right leg was numb. Pinched a nerve, she thought. Stretch it out, keep moving.

Glass opened the Saturn's trunk, took out a red plastic five-gallon gasoline container. Cordell got out of the van, came around to the back, uncertain what to do.

"Get that other trunk open," Glass said to him. "We need to finish up here."

Larry stowed the tac bag in the Saturn's trunk. They'd agreed the money would go in one car, the equipment in the other. She and Larry would take the Toyota and the cash, Cordell and Glass the Saturn and the guns.

Glass climbed back up into the van with the gas can, pushed the duffel out. Larry carried it to the Toyota's open trunk, dropped it in, and shut the lid. Glass began splashing fuel around inside the van, the harsh smell of it drifting out.

She felt Cordell beside her, turned to him. "How you doing?"

"I'm all right."

"You did okay out there."

He didn't respond. Glass climbed down, tossed the empty can inside. He had a dull red road flare in his hand.

"You two go first," he said to her. "We'll see you back there."

She went to the Toyota, stamped her right foot on the ground twice to speed up the circulation, feeling pins and needles in her leg now. Larry looked at her across the roof, said, "You okay to drive?"

"Good enough." She got behind the wheel. Multicolored wires hung from the cracked steering column. She braided two together, and the engine started.

Larry got in beside her. "You sure?"

"I'm sure," she said. "Let's get out of here."

They went slowly up the driveway. The Lexus was in the garage, the door shut. She backed the Toyota up next to Larry's rental, pulled wires apart, and the engine went quiet.

They sat there, waiting for the Saturn, listening to the wind. The rain had slackened, but the clouds were low and dark. The pain in her back was a steady throbbing.

"Got crazy back there," he said.

"It did."

"I maybe killed that man. I don't know."

"If you hadn't shot him, he would have killed me."

"Could have gone a lot worse, I guess."

"Always," she said. "Come on, let's have a look, see what we've got."

They got out, and she opened the trunk, unzipped the duffel. The money was in thick packs, some of them bound by plain rubber bands.

"Sloppy," he said. She took out a pack, looked through it. Hundreds and fifties, but worn bills. That was good. She shook the bag, looking for anything else that wasn't money, found nothing.

They turned as the Saturn came up the driveway, Glass at the wheel. He parked beside the Toyota. She put the bills back, zipped the bag shut, started to pull it from the trunk, felt a surge of pain. Larry saw it in her face.

"I've got it," he said. "Go on in." He took out the bag, shut the lid.

Inside the house, it was almost dark as night. There was a half inch of water on the kitchen floor. They went into the living room, and he dropped the duffel on the couch. The wind picked up outside, rattled something upstairs.

Glass and Cordell came in, shaking off the rain, Cordell carrying the bag with the weapons.

"How'd we do?" Glass said. He smelled of gasoline and smoke.

"Waiting on you before we find out," she said.

"You all right?"

"I'm good."

Cordell set the tac bag clanking on the floor. Glass switched on the lanterns, went to the bay window and looked back down to the street. "Nobody out there."

"Good," Larry said. "Let's do the count."

"First things first," Glass said, and took an empty tac bag from behind the couch, opened it on the floor. "Give it up. Any other weapons. Vests and masks, whatever else you have. Cell phones, too."

Larry took off his windbreaker, then shrugged out of the sweater, unsnapped his vest. Glass was doing the same. Her own vest had been left behind in the van. She left the Glock where it was.

Cordell hadn't moved. He stood behind the couch, watching them.

"Come on," Glass said. "Vest off. I'm ditching them." He folded his own vest into the tac bag. Larry dropped his on top, pulled the windbreaker back on.

"Getting kind of used to it," Cordell said.

"Take it off," Glass said. Then to Crissa, "You ready to count?"

"Yeah."

Glass pulled a folding chair near the couch, sat, and unzipped the duffel. Larry took the other chair, sat close by. Glass began taking out money, lining the packs up on the coffee table. They soon ran out of space, had to set packs on the floor, Glass counting, then handing them over to Larry, who counted them again.

Cordell had his windbreaker off, was pulling the sweater over his head. He looked at the money, glasses askew, said, "Fat stacks."

"No way it's a half mil," Larry said. "But it's two hundred K at least."

"Three hundred, I'm betting," Glass said. "Or close."

Cordell was fumbling with the vest straps. He got it off finally, draped it on the back of the couch. Beneath it, he wore the same Bob Marley T-shirt she'd seen before, now dark with sweat across the stomach. He pushed his glasses back up on his nose, watched them count.

"Have a seat," she told him. "This could take a while." Glass had a small calculator out, was punching in numbers.

Her back ached. She wanted to sit down but was afraid she wouldn't be able to get up again. She rubbed the small of her back, resettled the Glock. When they were done with the split, ready to leave, she'd put it in the bag with the other guns.

"Three twenty-five," Glass said. "Even."

"My count, too," Larry said.

To Glass, she said, "Five thousand off the top to you, like we agreed. Then that's ninety thousand to each of us."

"You were always quick that way," he said. "Cordell and I are going to hang here a bit, let you two get clear. Leave your shares in the duffel, it'll be easier to carry. Just get rid of the bag when you can, to be safe."

"Right," Larry said, and began loading money back into the bag.

Glass looked at her. "Nice work."

"It was," she said, and then the ceiling above them creaked.

They all looked up. She reached back, touched the Glock, turned and saw Cordell. He met her eyes, and in that instant she knew. Then his hand was coming out from behind his back, from under the Bob Marley T-shirt, and there was a gun in it.

She dove to her left, hit the table, then the floor, packs of money flying around her. She got the Glock free, was bringing it around, but Cordell was already firing, the gun jumping in his hands. Glass spun, as if turning away from the shots.

She kicked at the table to get clear of it. Glass fell across her, and she saw the red and black hole under his right cheekbone. She pushed him away, saw Larry dive for the bag with the guns, Cordell still firing. Then there were footsteps on the stairs, and someone else there in the shadows, firing down over the railing at them.

She snapped a shot at the stairs, then kicked the lantern closest to her. It hit the wall and went dark, and she fired in Cordell's direction, kept rolling, knocking over the chairs, the room full of gunfire.

She came up in a crouch below the bay window, her back to the wall, fired at Cordell again—too low—saw the bullet strike the vest on the back of the couch. She fired higher, but he was already dropping down. The bullet broke glass somewhere beyond him.

She saw the second lantern beside the couch, fired at it. Metal spanged, and it flew to the side. The room dropped into darkness.

More muzzle flashes came from the stairs, rounds striking the wall behind her. She fired at the flashes, raised up for a better shot, and then Larry was coming toward her out of the dark, moving fast. He slammed into her, an arm around her waist, and they went backward through the window, glass and wood giving way around them.

They crashed into skeletal shrubs, then hard onto solid ground, the breath going out of her, the Glock flying from her hand. Larry was already scrambling to his feet, reaching for her, but she pulled away from him, lunged for the gun in the dirt, got it just as a silhouette appeared at the window. She fired at it, and then it was gone again.

"Come on," Larry said, and she turned to see he had the duffel slung over his left shoulder. He'd had it with him when they'd gone through the window. Their money.

She fired again into the dark window, then rolled to her feet on the wet ground, started across the driveway at a run, Larry beside her. Cover ahead, dead hedges bordering the next yard.

As they reached them, there were popping sounds behind, more shots from the house. Larry fell to his knees. She stood above him, twisted, the Glock in a two-handed grip, and began to fire at the window. Three shots and the slide locked back, the magazine empty.

He was struggling to his feet, out of breath. She dropped the gun, grabbed his arm, and then they were pushing through the hedges together. One of the duffel's straps snagged on a branch, and he pulled to try to free it, the bushes shaking.

"Leave it," she said.

"No way." The strap came loose all at once, and he started to fall again. She caught his windbreaker, pushed and pulled him through the rest of the hedge and into the next yard.

The house here was almost identical to the one they'd left, dark, the windows and front door boarded over. No place to hide. Behind them, two more pops, wild shots. Still gripping his jacket, she pulled him along as they ran. On the other side of the yard was a blacktop driveway, then a low stone wall, trees beyond.

She slipped on the wet ground, landed hard, and then he was pulling her up. They crossed the yard together. She reached the wall first, rolled over the top, thumped into the dirt below. He came over behind her, landed on her with a grunt, drove the breath from her again. They rolled clear of each other, and she came up onto her knees, keeping her head below the level of the wall.

Another shot sounded behind them, but muffled, fired inside the house this time, not through the window. Then two more. Then silence.

Larry was breathing hard, his face pale.

"That little prick," he said. "I should have known."

"We need to keep moving."

"You hit anybody back there?"

"I don't know. But we're not going to wait around to find out."

He rolled onto his knees and winced with pain. It was then she saw the smear of blood on the back of his jacket.

"You're hit," she said.

"Caught one back there. Maybe two. I don't know."

They were on a corner lot, no house here, just unbroken trees, open street on two sides. To their left was a chain-link fence, beyond it a long low garage, some sort of municipal facility. Against the side wall of the garage were a half-dozen black plastic fifty-five-gallon drums. Gang tags on the walls, broken windows. The building empty and dark.

She peered over the top of the wall, back at the house. No movement. No noise. But Cordell and his partner would come looking for them soon.

She nodded at the chain-link fence. "Can you climb that?"

"Maybe. I doubt it."

"We have to," she said. "We can't be out in the open like this. They'll find us."

"I can try."

She helped him to his feet, and they moved in a crouch toward the fence. He dragged the duffel behind him. The back of his jacket was dark with blood now. She could see the hole in the material, just above his right hip, where the bullet had gone in.

He saw her looking, said, "I'm okay. It doesn't hurt. Not yet. I didn't see what happened to Charlie. Did you?"

"Yes," she said, and left it at that.

The fence was about eight feet high, with two strands of barbed wire across the top. No razor wire, at least. The front gate of the fenced lot was chained and padlocked. Once inside, they might be safe.

"What do you think?" she said.

"I don't know."

"We have to try."

"Leave me. Take the money."

"No."

Faint noises from back at the house. Car doors shutting, an engine starting.

"We don't have much time," she said. "We can make it if we do it together. It's not that high."

"Looks pretty fucking high to me."

"We have to move."

She took off the windbreaker, tied the sleeves around her

waist. She backed up a few feet, got a running start, leaped, and caught the fence about halfway up, the chain-link rattling and swaying under her. She locked gloved fingers through metal diamonds, got the toe of her boot into another, pulled herself up, and began to climb. The pain in her back was gone now, along with the numbness in her leg. There was nothing but the fence, the yard beyond.

Near the top, she clung with one hand, untied the sleeves of the jacket with the other. Just the two strands of rusty barbed wire, no Y-bar to keep someone from climbing over. But the wire could catch her just as easily, hang her up there, draw blood.

She swung the windbreaker over her head. It took two tries to get it draped across the wire, lining side up.

She looked down at Larry, reached. "Come on, I'll help you."

"I don't think I can do it."

Headlights coming down the street now, slow.

"Climb," she said.

He bent to pick up the duffel, fell to one knee.

"Forget the money," she said. "Come on."

He shook his head, stood, hoisted the bag with both hands, unsteady, pushed it up toward her.

There was no time to argue. When the bag was high enough, she hooked fingers in the strap, got the duffel up and onto the barbed wire, then tipped it over. It landed in weeds on the other side.

She looked back down, and he was already climbing, the fence moving under him. He lost his grip on the wet chain-link, slid down, then started up again. She reached for him, caught his jacket, pulled up. He was gasping for air, moving slow, the adrenaline wearing off, the pain and fatigue setting in. She looked back toward the street. If the car came around the corner now, they'd both be outlined against the fence, easy targets.

Halfway up, he stopped, hung there with both hands. She hooked a hand into his armpit, then got her forearm under him to take some of his weight.

"Almost there," she said.

He grimaced with pain, kept climbing. She had his belt now, could hold him steady as he climbed past her. He reached the top, got his right leg across the jacket, teetered there for a moment and almost fell. Then he righted himself, swung his left leg over and began to climb down the other side. Three feet from the ground, he lost his grip, fell, grunted when he hit the dirt.

Headlights shining through the trees. She went over the top fast, started down, pulling the jacket after her. It snagged on a barb, then tore free. She let it go, dropped the last few feet, landed hard on her side in weeds. He started to get up, and she grabbed his jacket, hissed, "Stay down." He flattened himself beside her. Thunder echoed in the distance.

The car had stopped around the corner and parked at an angle, headlight beams cutting through the trees. They'd have the windows down, watching and listening. The high beams switched on, threw shadows against the side of the garage. She laid her cheek on wet ground

Would they get out, search the corner lot on foot? Thunder rumbled again, and the rain came harder, slanting down out of the gray sky. The car backed away, straightened, drove on.

A window of time now, maybe a minute before the car rounded the corner, came down past the front gate. She looked at the garage, the bay doors, most of the glass panels missing. The right-hand door wasn't closed completely. There was a foot-high gap between the bottom of the door and the bay floor.

She pointed at it, and he nodded. She grabbed her jacket, moved in a crouch toward the door, dragging the duffel behind her. She bent beside the door, pushed the duffel and jacket through the gap, then waved for him to follow her. Headlights out front now. She wedged a shoulder under the door, forced it up another few inches, the mechanism rusty.

He sprinted toward the garage, slipped and fell, then got up again. At the bay door, he dropped to his stomach and crawled through. She pulled him in the rest of the way, then rolled clear of the door.

They lay on concrete, panting in the darkness. Water dripped from the ceiling. In the shadows around her, she could see discarded tires, empty oil cans.

"Stay down," she said. "I'm going to take a look."

"Careful." He dragged himself along the floor, got his back against a wall. He sat up, pulled the duffel into his lap, breathing heavy. "Christ, it's cold."

She rose slowly, her knees aching, stood in profile, and looked through one of the broken panes. The car had pulled up to the gate, headlights lighting up the front of the garage, wipers swishing. It was the Lexus.

"That them?" Larry said.

"Yeah."

"They see us?"

"I don't think so."

The driver's door opened, and Cordell got out. He had a gun in one hand, a flashlight in the other. She pulled back from the glass but kept him in sight. Larry's breathing seemed to fill the room.

Cordell played the flashlight along the gate, then tucked the light under one arm, rattled the chain that held the gate shut.

"This lock's old," he said. "Ain't nobody in here."

The passenger door opened. A black man about Cordell's age got out. He wore a dark hoodie, had one hand pressed against the left side of his stomach. The other hand held a gun down by his side. He leaned on the hood of the car for support. At least one of her rounds had found its mark, but hadn't done enough damage to stop him.

She looked around, hoping for a tire iron, a chain, a length of pipe, anything she could use if they came inside. She'd go straight at them, do what damage she could, try to get one of their weapons, hurt them as much as possible before they put her down.

Cordell turned to the other one. "What you think?"

"Fuck it, man, let's go. I'm hurting. They still around here somewhere. We'll find them."

Cordell shone his flashlight at the bay door. She pulled back, saw the beam illuminate broken shards of glass in the panes, then pass along the gap at the bottom of the door. He rattled the chain again.

"Yeah," he said. "Fuck it."

The light went out. Then the sound of doors closing, the car backing up. The headlights passed over the front of the garage a final time as they drove away, the engine noise growing fainter. She watched through the window, saw their taillights moving down the street.

She let out her breath, looked down at Larry. He had his arms around the duffel.

"They're gone," she said. "But they'll be back before long. When they can't find us on the street, they'll come back this way."

When he didn't respond, she said, "Are you all right?" Realized then she couldn't hear his breathing anymore.

"Larry?"

She knelt beside him. His eyes were open, glassy. She pulled off a glove, touched the left side of his throat, knew already what she'd find. The skin still warm there, but no pulse, no movement.

Wind and rain rattled the bay doors. She sank down beside him, her back to the wall, closed her eyes. When she opened them again, they were stinging.

Thunder again, but farther away. She shivered, felt the cold in her bones.

She couldn't risk being out on the street, didn't know when they'd circle back. There was nothing to do but wait until night. She pulled her glove back on, blinked away the wetness in her eyes.

She found her jacket there in the darkness, torn but whole. She put it on, zipped it high. Then she wrapped her arms around her knees, pulled in tight for warmth.

She closed her eyes, sat beside Larry's body, and listened to the wind.

SEVEN

Fifteen minutes later, the Lexus came back from the opposite direction, cruised slow up the street, threw headlights on the front of the garage again. They were backtracking, trying to find where she and Larry had gone to ground.

She stood, legs cramping, leaned against the wall. Through the broken glass, she could see the Lexus out there, both of them sitting inside, thinking it over.

Almost night now, and no lights on the outside of the building. She was safe in here, out of sight, as long as they didn't come in.

She watched, waiting, while they made up their minds. Then the Lexus backed out again, went to the corner and made a right at the wooded lot, headed back toward the house.

She gave it another ten minutes, in case it was a trap, the two of them parked around the corner, headlights off, waiting for her to show herself. Or coming back this way again, with bolt cutters for the gate chain.

She'd laid Larry out as gently as she could on the floor. Looking down at him, she had a sudden memory of the day they'd first met. He and Wayne playing cards at the house in Delaware, laughing and drinking, when she came in. He was an old friend, Wayne had told her, from back in the day. She'd guessed what that meant, and she hadn't been wrong. A week later, they were prepping the Houston job. And then everything had gone to hell.

She took off her glove again, to close his eyes. No light there now. Just a husk, she told herself. The man inside is gone.

She pushed the duffel under the bay door, crawled out after it. The rain had stopped, and she could see the glow of the moon through the clouds.

Two of the drums on the side of the building were lidless, filled with trash, oil cans, and plastic bottles. She tipped one over, water and garbage spilling out. With the barrel half empty, she righted it again, wedged the duffel down into it, covered it with trash. She kicked away the garbage left on the ground.

It hurt to go back over the fence. Her joints were stiff, and her feet slipped from the wet links. There was no strength in her legs. She'd considered looking for a tool to break the lock on the front gate, go out that way. But she didn't want to leave a sign someone had been there.

On the other side, she limped into the cover of the trees, knelt at the stone wall, and looked back toward the house. As she watched, the Lexus came fast down the driveway, hit the street, fishtailed, sped away in the opposite direction.

The smell of smoke. Flickering light in the bay window, then a gout of flame bloomed through it, began to crawl up the outer wall. Gasoline, she thought, and another of Glass's road flares.

There was light in other windows now, too, the house full of flames, dark smoke pouring out. They would have left Charlie's body there, maybe doused it with gas first. The fire would cover their tracks, destroy any evidence they'd left behind.

Flames rose in the backyard. They'd torched the cars as well. She heard the flat *crump* of a gas tank going up, then another. There would be sirens soon, police, firefighters. She couldn't stay here.

A loud *crack* sounded from the house, and part of the roof gave, sparks rising up into the column of smoke. Flames began to lick out into the open air.

She sat back against the wall, trying to gather her strength. She was soaked to the bone, stiff and sore. Slowly, she got to her feet, one hand on the wall for support. Pain was deep in her hips and knees.

To the west, she could see the glow of the city reflected in the overcast. There'd be no cabs around here, no cars on the street to hotwire.

The rain had moved on. She saw flashes of lightning in the clouds above the city. How many miles away? No way to tell. And nothing for it. She walked.

* * *

She kept to the shadows just off the street, ready to hide if she saw headlights. She was limping, hips and back aching with every step, but the exertion warmed her, drove out some of the chill.

After a while she came to a block where the houses were lit, the yards small but neat. Urban homesteaders, gentrification on its way. A Honda Civic was parked at the curb. She looked in the driver's window, saw a locking bar across the steering wheel, a blinking red light on the dash. She walked on.

There was a party on the next block. A two-story house with all the windows lit, music coming out, voices. The driveway was full, cars lining both sides of the street.

She watched from a stand of trees on the corner. Headlights came toward her, and she backed farther into the shadows. The car passed her, pulled to the curb a half block away. A couple in their thirties—the man white, the woman black—got out, the woman carrying a bottle of wine. The man locked the car behind them, and they went up the driveway to a side door of the house. The door opened for them, music and laughter spilling out.

She ran gloved fingers through her damp hair, knowing how she must look. The jacket was reversible, so she turned it inside out to hide the worst of the rips and stains. She brushed twigs and mud from her jeans, zipped the jacket higher. Then she crossed the street, walked up the driveway.

She went in without knocking, into a warm kitchen crowded with people. Trays of cold cuts and bread on the table, a sideboard crowded with liquor bottles, Sinatra coming from speakers somewhere.

People glanced at her, then turned back to their own conversations. They were all in their thirties, early forties, young professionals. She smiled as best she could, wound her way through them, took a wine bottle from the sideboard as she passed. The living room was just as crowded, the music louder here. A woman in a black dress and pearls looked at the bottle and said, "You must be psychic."

Crissa handed it to her. "Bathroom?"

"Upstairs. Second door on the right." The woman looked at her more closely. "Honey, you look like you've had a rough night."

Crissa went by her and up the carpeted staircase. In the hallway, three people stood outside the closed bathroom door. At the end of the corridor a door was half open, light on inside.

She went in, and it was what she hoped. A bedroom, coats laid out on the bedspread. She eased the door shut behind her, started going through pockets. There was a set of Hyundai keys in the second coat she searched. She pocketed them, caught a glimpse of herself in a wall mirror. Her hair was matted and tangled, her face scratched in half a dozen places.

She went back into the hallway, forced a smile for the trio outside the bathroom, caught a whiff of marijuana from inside.

Back downstairs, the woman in black watching her now. Crissa nodded at her, went through the kitchen and out the side door.

On the street, she got out the keys, pressed the UNLOCK button. A half block down, a white Elantra beeped and flashed its lights.

She walked to it, got behind the wheel, started the engine. As she pulled away from the curb, she looked back at the house. No one had come out after her.

She waited a block until she popped on the headlights. Then she made a left, followed by another left, headed back the way she'd come.

There was a single fire truck outside the house, sending a stream of water into an upstairs window. No flames now, but gray smoke still billowing up. A Detroit Metro SUV was parked behind the fire truck, rollers on, their light reflected in the run-off water coursing down the gutter. Two uniformed officers stood beside it, looking up at the house, bored. They turned to watch her as she drove past.

She went up two blocks, then doubled back on a parallel street, headlights off, and drove back to the garage. The padlock on the front gate was intact. There was no sign anyone else had been there.

She parked on the sidewalk, left the engine running, got out. The air smelled of smoke.

There was a spare-tire kit in the trunk, a short-handled tire iron. She carried it to the gate, slipped the shaft into the rusty chain, wedged one end against a crossbar, then pulled hard with both hands. On the third pull, a link snapped, and the chain rattled loose. She threaded it through the gate, tossed it aside.

The hinges were rusty, squealing as she shouldered the gate open. The duffel was where she'd left it. She pulled it out of the drum, and for the first time noticed the hole on one side of the bag, a larger one on the other. A bullet had gone straight through.

She slung the strap over her shoulder, looked at the bay door. He's gone, she thought. And it could have played out another way just as easily, you lying dead in there, or back in the house. But he'd gotten her out of there, just as he'd gotten Wayne out of that car in Houston.

She went back through the gate, put the duffel and tire iron in the trunk, shut it. Low thunder sounded in the west. She pulled back onto the street and drove away.

On the edge of the city, she found a phone booth outside a convenience store, called 911. She gave the location of the garage as best she could, said she'd seen men inside, heard gunshots. The operator was still asking questions when Crissa hung up. It had been risky to call, but she couldn't leave him there, forgotten, alone.

At the airport, she parked the Elantra in a long-term lot, caught a shuttle bus to her hotel. She carried the duffel up to her room, left it on the bed.

The tremors were on her now. She undressed, showered in water as hot as she could stand, then sat in the tub, let the spray rain down on her. She closed her eyes, all of it running through her mind again. The punch of the AK round into her back. Gunshots in the dark. Larry bent over the duffel in the shadowed garage, still and silent. Charlie Glass, shot through the face, falling across her.

After a while, the pain in her back and hips began to fade. She was calmer now; the shaking had stopped. She turned off the water, toweled dry, wiped steam from the mirror and twisted to look at her back. There was a softball-sized bruise under her right shoulder blade, purple in the center, yellow at the edges. Not enough pain for a broken rib. She'd been lucky.

She dressed in sweatpants and T-shirt, then unzipped the duffel and spilled money out onto the bed. She pulled up a chair and began to count.

A hundred and sixty thousand in the bag. So the count they'd done at the house had been good. Eighty thousand of it was Larry's share. It belonged to his people, if she could find them.

She went to the window, looked out at the night. Cordell and his partner were out there somewhere. Her fatigue was giving way to anger, at what they'd done, at herself for not reading the signs beforehand. For being too slow, for letting it all fall apart around her. For the deaths of two good men.

But there was nothing she could do about any of that now, nothing more to be gained here. She'd gotten away clean, with her share of the money. It would make no sense to go after them for the rest, even if she could find them. And there was little chance they'd come after her. They were amateurs who'd gotten lucky. They wouldn't know where to start.

It was over. Time to go home.

She put the money back in the duffel, then stretched out on the bed, turned off the light, knew she wouldn't be able to sleep. She still lay like that, eyes open, when pale dawn filled the window.

EIGHT

Burke lost his last three hundred betting the pass line on a black kid in his twenties who'd been shooting hot for the last fifteen minutes. Players were elbow-to-elbow at the table, had migrated over from other games, drawn by the shouts, hoping to get in on the streak while the kid was still golden.

Burke watched the red dice bounce across green felt, strike the far wall, and fall back. Snake eyes.

"*Got*damn," the kid said, and a moan seemed to come up from the other players. The stickman raked in the chips, Burke's three black ones among them, said, "New shooter," and looked at him. Burke was on the kid's left, so the next roll would go to him. He shook his head.

He'd walked in the door with three grand, had started strong at roulette, then blackjack. An hour later, he'd been up five thousand, but then the whole thing had started to go south on him. He'd moved on to craps, hoping to catch some of the kid's fire, but had brought his bad luck along with him.

Burke turned away, got out his cigarettes. A hollow-eyed man in overalls and John Deere cap elbowed past him, took his place at the table.

Burke moved through the casino toward the bar, music and electronic sounds blaring from the banks of slot machines. He lit his tenth Newport of the day, snapped the lighter closed, dropped it in the pocket of his suit coat, fished out his silver money clip. Two twenties and a five. Time to call it a night.

The barmaid was a heavy blonde in a white shirt, red vest, sleeve garters. He took a stool, and she set a tin ashtray in front of him. "Maker's Mark," he said, "ice," and put a twenty on the bar.

The barmaid brought his drink, took his money. He tapped ash from the Newport, looked at his Rolex. Nine P.M., but it felt like midnight.

When the barmaid brought his change, he pushed two singles toward her, took a pull from his drink. A voice close by said, "Easy to lose track of time in here, isn't it?"

He looked to his left. Two stools down was a woman in her early thirties, red hair piled high, green shimmery dress, small spangled purse under one arm. Working girl, he thought. The suit drew them every time.

"Easy enough," he said.

"What's that you're drinking?"

He told her.

"I'm more of a Jack Daniel's girl myself." She moved onto

the stool beside him. He could smell her perfume now, sandalwood. She took a pack of Pall Malls from her purse, gingerly pulled one out between long fingernails. "Simple girl. Simple tastes."

He got out his lighter. She put the cigarette between her lips, leaned forward. As he lit it for her, she touched his hand. She straightened, blew smoke to the side, said, "Thanks."

"How's your night going?" he said.

"Could be better. Yours?"

"Same here. But I'm hoping for an improvement."

She gave that a smile. The barmaid came over. "Jack on the rocks," the redhead said, then to Burke, "I'm Lucinda." She held out a hand. "Like the singer."

He shook it. The palm was cool and dry. "Frank."

"Anybody ever call you Frankie? You never hear that anymore."

"Not since I was a kid."

When the barmaid came back with the drink, he put his other twenty on the bar, watched her take it.

"Cheers," Lucinda said, and they clinked glasses. She leaned forward until their shoulders brushed, didn't pull back.

The bourbon went down warm, lit up his stomach, Burke remembering then he hadn't eaten since lunch.

"What do you play?" she said.

"Little of everything. You?"

"Me? I guess I'm more of a watcher."

He gave her the smile. "You're all about the ambience, huh?"

"That's me."

She took a pull from the cigarette, set it in the ashtray beside his. Up close, she looked younger. A hard twenty-five, maybe. Too much eye makeup, trying to cover up the first traces of crow's-feet.

"Can I ask you something, Frank?"

"Sure." Knowing what was coming.

"Are you a cop? Nothing against them. I just want to know."

"Do I look like a cop?"

"Honestly? A little."

"I used to be. Detroit Metro."

"I knew it. I can always tell."

"Used to be."

"When was that?"

"That I left? Five years. Almost six."

"You retired?"

"Something like that."

"You look too young for that."

"I'm older than you think."

She touched his arm. "You can tell me to mind my own business. I won't mind."

"It's all right."

"What do you do now?"

"Private."

"What's that mean?"

"Security work," he said. "Insurance fraud, employee theft, that sort of thing."

"For the casinos?"

"Sometimes. I'm a subcontractor, put it that way. Businesses, individuals. Kind of a troubleshooter, I guess. Pretty boring work. Mostly."

"Mostly?" She smiled. Her knee touched his. "You carry a gun?"

"Only when I have to. Most times, a gun gets you into a lot more trouble than it can get you out of."

"How about now?"

He shook his head. "I have a concealed carry permit, but you can't bring them into the casinos anyway."

She clinked the ice in her glass, traced the rim with an index finger.

"So let me ask you, Frank." She moved in closer. "You through throwing your money away for the night?" She sucked the fingertip.

"Maybe."

"Looking to party?"

"Could be." He sipped his drink, gave her the smile again.

"You in this hotel?" she said.

"No. The Hilton. Up the street."

"Where do you live?"

"Grosse Pointe," he lied. "Out near the lake."

"Pretty fancy for an ex-cop."

"I do all right."

She slid from the stool, balancing on high heels, got her purse from the bar. "Well, what do you say, Frankie?"

He finished his drink. "I say let's go."

* * *

He got his overcoat from the checkroom, and they stood outside under the neon while the valet brought the Impala around. Burke tipped him the five. Now he was down to just singles.

The rain had stopped, but the streets were slick, and there was thunder somewhere far off. He lit another cigarette in the car, cracked the window to blow out smoke. He felt pleasantly light-headed.

"Nice car," she said. "It looks new."

"It is." They drove on.

"You sure this is the way to the Hilton?" she said.

"Yeah, up Lafayette, then right on Brush. You've been there, right?"

"I don't remember going this way."

The blocks grew darker, the restaurants and bars thinning out. He made the turn onto Brush and then the left onto Gratiot, the Hilton in sight now, up at the brightly lit corner.

Ahead on the right was a redbrick factory building, and an empty parking lot, a billboard there promising affordable condos to come.

"I usually park in there," he said. "It's free."

She took a cell phone from her purse. "I have to make a call."

"Who to?"

She punched in a number, raised the phone to her left ear.

"Don't be rude," he said, and slapped it from her hand.

The phone hit the dashboard, clattered off and landed at her feet.

"What . . ." she started to say, and he jerked the wheel, pulled into the dark parking lot, drove into the shadows at the back, and hit the brakes hard. She rocked forward against the shoulder harness. He killed the headlights, turned the engine off.

"What the fuck is wrong with you?" she said.

He knew there was more coming, didn't want to hear it. He backhanded her in the face, and she pulled away, hit her head against the window. She raised a hand to protect herself, clawed at the door latch with the other. He grabbed her left wrist, squeezed hard, said, "Stop it."

She'd backed as far as she could against the door. He held her thin wrist tight in his hand, pushed his cigarette out through the crack in the window, unsnapped his seat belt. The faint glow of a streetlamp lit the inside of the car.

"You're thinking about screaming," he said. "But that would be a mistake. All it'll get you is a broken arm."

"Let go of me." Fear in her eyes for the first time.

He squeezed tighter, felt her bones. "I might. Or not. That's up to you. Give me that phone."

When she didn't move, he twisted her arm, bent her forward. She gasped with pain. He held her there, her elbow locked. "Remember what I said."

She picked up the phone with her free hand. He let go of her wrist, took it. She straightened, jerked her arm away. His fingers left bright red marks on her skin.

"Just sit your ass right there," he said. He looked at the phone. "Who'd you call?"

She rubbed her arm, back to the door. "A friend."

There were numbers on the display, but the call hadn't gone through. He pressed the power button, watched the phone go dark, set it on the dash. "Purse."

"You're still a cop, aren't you?"

He didn't answer. Let her think what she wanted.

Inside the purse was a wallet, a package of Kleenex, three keys on a chain, her cigarettes and a plastic lighter, four condoms in gold foil. He opened the wallet. Three bills inside, a hundred and two fifties.

"You didn't have such a bad night," he said. He folded the money, put it in his overcoat pocket, got out her driver's license. She was younger in the photo, straight hair parted in the middle, darker than it was now. Lou Ann Crumlin, with an address in Livonia.

"You're right," he said. "Lucinda's better. Now I know where you live, Lou Ann."

He went through the wallet. A single credit card and a picture of a boy, maybe five years old.

"Yours?" he said.

When she didn't answer, he looked at her. There were tears in her eyes, mascara starting to streak. "Answer me, honey."

"Yes. He's mine."

"How old?"

"Six."

"Good for you. What's his name?"

She looked away, but he knew she wouldn't try to escape. They'd passed that point. He'd broken her.

"Alexander," she said.

"Good-looking kid. He live with you?"

She nodded, couldn't face him.

"That's too bad." He put everything back into the purse, dropped it at her feet. "It must be rough, growing up with a mother who's out selling her ass every night."

She reached for the purse, and he looked down the front of her dress, caught a flash of black lace bra. He thought about taking one of those condoms, pulling her out of the car, doing her facedown over the hood. But he couldn't be sure someone wouldn't come along, use the lot to make a U-turn, see them there.

When she reached for the phone, he slapped her wrist. "No."

She flinched, drew back.

"Ask you a question, Lou Ann. How come I've never seen you around before? Was a time I knew every girl working every hotel in Detroit. Even the ones over the bridge in Windsor. But you're a new face."

"What do you want?"

"You haven't been in the Life long, have you? I can tell. Look at it this way, I'm doing you a favor. You'll be smarter next time. Now take your shit and get out of here."

She fumbled to close her purse, couldn't get the catch to snap.

"Next time I run into you, though . . . hey, look at me or I'll crack you again . . . Next time I run into you, you better have more green to cough up than you had this time. This is my city, honey. You want to run with the big dogs, you have to pay."

He got out the Newports, lit one, nodded at her door. "Git."

"My phone."

"Don't push it. Go on, get out of here. I'm sick of that perfume."

She held the purse to her chest, pulled at the door latch. As she got out, he leaned to his left, brought his right foot up and shoved. She tumbled out onto the blacktop.

Her license had fallen onto the floor. He picked it up, scaled it out after her. "Don't forget this."

She was on her hands and knees, trying to get to her feet, sobbing softly, but not wanting him to see it. He leaned over, pulled the door shut, started the engine. She backed away from the car, tripped and fell again, sat there on the blacktop, crying.

He swung the Impala around, pulled out of the lot and back onto Gratiot. Two blocks later, he powered down the window, tossed out her phone.

Two hundred in his pocket, and the night was young. He could go back to the hotel, try his luck at craps again, maybe a few hands of blackjack, see where the night took him. But he was restless now, didn't know if he had the patience.

The cell phone in his coat pocket began to vibrate. He got it out, looked at the number, pushed SEND, and raised it to his ear. "Yeah."

On the other end of the line, Marquis Johnson said, "We need to talk."

If Marquis was calling, it meant he had trouble he couldn't handle on his own. And that kind of trouble meant money.

"You at the place?" Burke said.

"Yeah."

"On my way," Burke said, and ended the call. His luck had changed tonight after all.

NINE

The man who blocked Burke's path was a foot taller than him and fifty pounds heavier. Shaved head, and a scar that ran from the corner of his mouth to his ear. He gestured for Burke to raise his arms.

Burke shook his head. "I don't think so, brother."

"You want to go in or not?"

Burke looked past him to the door. It was steel, painted brown to look like wood. The kind of door that would hold up to a Stinger ram just long enough for someone on the other side to flush dope or slam a safe shut, spin the dial.

"Are we going to have an issue here?" Burke said. "Because I'm not in the mood."

The door opened, and Damien leaned out into the hall. "Yo, Luther, what's the holdup?"

"I'm trying to check the man, but he acting all hard."

"Man, forget that shit," Damien said. He opened the door wider. He wore a white silk jacket over a salmon-colored shirt. Burke could see the butt of a chromed automatic in his waistband.

Luther held Burke's eyes for a moment, then stepped aside. Burke went past him and through the door. Damien shut it behind them.

Marquis sat at an oak desk that was too big for the room, fingers steepled, watching them. Behind him, big windows looked down on Terry Street, one flight below.

Damien double-locked the door, slid a police bar into place, then leaned against the wall.

"Haven't seen that one before," Burke said. "You bring in some new boys?"

"Long time since you been up in here," Marquis said. "Lots of new faces around." He gestured to the red leather chair in front of the desk. There was a chest-high green safe on one side of the room, filing cabinets, and on a table near the safe a money-counting machine. Marquis's desktop was clear except for a multiline phone, an open laptop computer, and a dark automatic sitting atop a glossy magazine.

Burke sat, nodded at the gun. "You expecting a war?"

"Should I be?"

Burke looked across the desk at him, remembering the skinny teenager who'd run the streets, doing errands for the real Gs. And here he was now, Marky Johnson from 'round the way, reborn as drug kingpin. Detroit, the city of new beginnings.

Burke looked at Damien, then back at Marquis. "Maybe

you need to backtrack a little," he said. "Because I have no idea what you're talking about."

Marquis glanced at Damien, then sat back. He wore wide aviator glasses with tinted lenses, powder blue shirt open to show a single gold chain. He was in his late thirties, old for the Game, on top longer than most.

Burke had known his father, a grifter and con man named St. Louis Slim. Burke had helped identify his body when they pulled it out of the river, his throat cut, two bullets in the back of his head. Still a patrolman then, Burke had gone to the family's house to deliver the news. Marquis was thirteen at the time, Damien ten.

"We got hit today," Marquis said.

"Let me guess. The drop-off? For the Mexicans?"

Marquis nodded. "You hear anything?"

Burke got out the Newports. "All news to me."

"Man, don't do that in here."

"You blow weed here all the time. I can smell it. What's the difference?"

"It's not the same. Those things right there'll kill you."

"Like that shit you sell on the street?"

"I sell it. I don't use it."

Burke put the pack on the desktop, then leaned forward and picked up the gun. Damien took a step away from the wall. Marquis didn't move.

Burke turned the gun over in his hand. It was a Beretta 92, shiny black steel, rubber grips. He ejected the magazine. Fourteen rounds.

"Careful with that," Marquis said.

"Nice weapon."

"You like it, I can get you one."

"No, thanks. I'm good. Not queer for them, like some people. Way I see it, a gun's a tool, like anything else." He slid the magazine back into the grip. "You think whoever ripped you today will keep coming at you? That it?"

"Maybe."

"You know anyone ready to war like that?"

"If you'd asked me yesterday, I'd say nobody had the stones."

Burke put the gun back on the desk, saw the title of the magazine.

"*Bloomberg Business Week,*" he said. "That's a good one. Detroit dope slingers have come a long way since the Chambers Brothers."

"The Chambers Brothers were punks. Country boys. In the right place at the right time, that's all."

"They had their day."

"Shit. When crack started, money was laying on the ground. All you had to do was pick it up. Didn't need to be no businessman. Things are different now."

"I guess they are," Burke said. "I miss those old days sometimes though. Maserati Rick. Young Boys. You knew who the players were back then."

"Yeah, everybody did. And where are they now?"

"I see your point."

"When I stepped up, there was some chaotic shit going on

here. You saw it. People warring, dropping bodies. Everybody dealing. Damien and I, we run those amateurs out. They either got on the team or they got gone."

"I know," Burke said. "You consolidated."

"Did what I had to, like any other CEO. Know the market. Cut your risks. Maximize the profit."

"Eliminate the competition."

"That, too."

"Seems to me I helped out some on that part."

"And got paid."

"And took a lot of risks. Busting other dealers, clearing the field for you? Letting you know when you had a witness problem? I'd say you got your money's worth."

There was a ceramic business card holder on the desk. Burke leaned forward, took a card. It read HARLEM RIVER MOTORS. MARQUIS JOHNSON, PRESIDENT AND CEO, with a phone number below, a 313 exchange.

He'll go legit someday, Burke thought. Funnel all that money into some other businesses, real estate. Play the CEO for real. And no room in that world for Burke. Marquis acting like he was slumming, by just sitting here talking to him. Looking down on Burke for taking his money, thinking the cash solved everything, smoothed over every disrespect.

"I get confused," Burke said. "Which way's the Harlem River from here?"

"Quit fucking around."

"All right." He put the card in a shirt pocket. "What happened?"

Burke shook out a Newport from the pack, listened. When

Marquis was done, Burke said, "Smoke grenades, huh? Son of a bitch." Thinking then, pros.

"Detroit PD was out there," Marquis said. "Don't know if they found anything else. You still have people you talk to there, right?"

Burke tapped the cigarette on the back of his hand. "Maybe. But nothing's free these days. Everybody wants to get paid."

"They will."

"Your guy that got hit. What kind of shape's he in?"

"He's at Detroit Receiving. In surgery last time Damien checked."

"I know him?"

"Willie Freeman. He been with me a long time."

"You trust them?"

"Who?"

"The boys in the Armada. Freeman, too."

"Far as it goes."

"You believe that story, the way they told it?"

"It fits. Damien went out to the scene afterwards, saw how it went down. Stories all match up. Why you making that face?"

"No easy way to say this."

"Go ahead."

"You fucked up, Marquis. Running a half-assed drop-off like that, something was bound to happen. I could have told you that."

"So maybe it was you."

"If it was, I wouldn't be sitting here right now. I'd be spending your money in Costa Rica."

"Not for long," Damien said behind him.

"Whoever took you off knew their shit," Burke said. "These weren't neighborhood gangbangers. Grenades, crash car. And they did it without dropping any bodies, except for your man."

"Meaning what?"

"It was a pro operation. Probably from out of town, with inside help. One of your people."

"Why you say that?"

"Think about it. How else would they know where the drop car was, when it would be there, what the setup was? They had all that shit down. Probably been watching your operation for weeks. How much they take you for?"

Marquis looked past him at Damien. "Enough."

"You don't want to tell me, I understand. But give me an idea what we're talking about here. Half a mil?"

Marquis shook his head. "Not that much."

"Then a quarter, at least. From what I can tell, bulk you've been buying lately, that has to be close. See, I know all your shit, too."

Marquis steepled his fingers again, watched him.

"Quarter million's a good day's work," Burke said. "They're probably on their way back to New York or Oklahoma or California, or wherever they came from, by now. You might find your inside man—if they haven't killed him already—but you won't get your money back. At least not on your own. And there's always the risk, six months later, they come back and do it again. Or somebody else with the same idea, thinking you're anybody's bitch now."

"That ain't gonna happen."

"Now you're talking out of your ass."

Marquis opened a desk drawer. Burke sat up, ready to close the distance, get hold of the Beretta if he needed to. Marquis smiled, put the gun in the drawer, shut it.

"I'll find them," Marquis said. "And I will get my money back."

"If you got this all wired already, why'd you call me?"

"I need somebody has access to Detroit PD. Can find out what they know and take it further, do what needs to be done."

"And that's me?"

"Isn't it?" Marquis dissing him because he knew he needed money, wouldn't have come here if he didn't.

He put the cigarette between his lips. "You know some of this is going to blow back on you anyway, right?"

"How you mean?"

"Your boys leave iron at the scene? Some of that will track back, serial numbers. Maybe fingerprints. Your man Willie, they'll be all over him, too, asking how he ended up in a firefight, wide-open street, middle of the afternoon."

"He'll keep his mouth shut. Say it was a drive-by, he was just a bystander."

"Might fly. Might not."

"What are you saying?"

"I'm saying you're right. I can find out all that shit you need. Might be there were witnesses, too, statements. I can make a phone call, have all that stuff an hour after it's typed up."

"That's a start."

"But I'd be sticking my neck out, calling in favors. Why would I want to do that?"

"We going to dance, or you going to name your price?"

"Just letting you know what you'd be paying for," Burke said. "Ballistics, forensics, fingerprints. Everything from that crime scene is going to come back at some point, and I'll have access to it. I'll take it from there, see where it all leads."

"All right. So you get that information, you bring it back to me, and then we talk about what it's worth."

"Doesn't work that way."

"How's it work?"

Burke took out the lighter, knowing he had him now. He lit the cigarette, snapped the lighter closed, put it away. Marquis opened another drawer, took out a glass ashtray, slid it across the desktop. Burke pulled it closer.

Marquis nodded at the cigarette. "Thought you'd quit those things. Weren't you sick a while back? What was it?"

Burke blew out smoke, met his eyes. "Cancer."

"What kind?"

"Prostate."

"And you still smoking."

"A man needs his vices."

"What'd you have? Chemo? Radiation?"

"Surgery." He ashed the cigarette in the tray.

"They cut it out of you?"

"Yeah."

"Can you still fuck?"

Burke looked at him for a moment, said, "I can still fuck your—"

Marquis raised a hand. "Don't. I shouldn't have asked."

"You keep that up, you'll make me say something that'll undo all the goodwill we've built over the years." He drew deep on the cigarette, felt the smoke in his lungs.

"So what's your plan?" Marquis said.

"I'd work it the way I'd work any case," Burke said, talking the smoke out. "I chase leads, knock on doors, look at evidence. Sooner or later, I'll have names. The crew who did this, they weren't first-timers. They'll have reps, MOs, sheets. Shake enough trees hard enough, you find out what you want."

"Then what?"

"Then I track them down, find what's left of your money, bring it back to you, and you give me a cut."

"What's left? I'm supposed to be happy with that?"

"There's a small window of time here to get anything back at all. You know that. I'd need to move fast."

"How much of a cut?"

"Half."

Marquis brushed a piece of dust off the desktop. "Half."

"Half is better than nothing. And nothing's what you've got right now."

Marquis was looking past him, at Damien again. Burke didn't turn. He tapped ash into the tray, waited.

Marquis looked back at him. "Even if you find the people that took my money, how do I know you'll bring it back to me?"

"I'd bring half back to you."

"Half, then. How do I know?"

"You don't. That's where our long professional relationship

comes into play. Mutual trust, right? I mean, if I wanted to, I could chase this whole thing down on my own, find them, keep all the money. You'd never know a thing about it."

"Why don't you?"

"Because you have information I need. I'll start with your people, pick up the threads, work from there. Finding your inside man—or woman—is the first step. I'll need your help with that." He blew out smoke.

"You are one arrogant white man, you know that?"

"I've been doing this shit my whole adult life. I know how to run an investigation. And that's what this is."

"Kind of arrogance put you in a hole in the ground."

"I've come this far," Burke said. "I'll take my chances."

A Detroit Metro cruiser flew by on the street below, light-bar flashing. They listened to the siren fade.

"If I say yes," Marquis said, "what do you need?"

"A list of names, and ten thousand up front."

"What names?"

"Everyone in the Armada, the driver of the drop-off car, anyone else who knew about the setup. For a start."

"Why you need the money?"

Burke stubbed the cigarette out in the ashtray. "I'll have expenses."

"Expenses. And that ten K, that comes out of your share after you find the money, right? If you find the money."

"That's right."

"Then answer me this: Why the fuck would I give you ten thousand dollars for something my own people will do for free, just because I tell them to?"

"Because I can promise results. You can throw a hundred soldiers on the street, and all of them together in a month couldn't do what I can in an hour. And ten grand to you is nothing. You make that before breakfast, right? But a quarter million, that's something else."

Marquis looked at Damien. "Cut him ten K out of the safe." Then to Burke, "Damien will be your man. Anything you need, you talk to him."

"I don't need anything else. Just the names. And the money."

"What happens if my boys out there looking, too, and they find those people—and my money—first?"

"Then I'd owe you ten thousand dollars, wouldn't I?"

"That's right," Marquis said. "You would."

Burke bought a pint of Four Roses on the way home, cracked it in the car. Back on the freeway, he took a long pull from the bottle, tucked it between his legs, and got out his cell. Rico answered on the first ring.

"Major Crimes. Sutton."

"How's the whitest black man in Detroit?"

"Ask your mother."

"Go fuck yourself."

"Would if I could."

"You pulling graveyard again? Who'd you piss off?"

"Everyone's hours are screwed up these days. Not enough warm bodies to go around in this broke-ass city. Can't make plans, can't do shit about it"

"I'm looking into something," Burke said. "Incident

downtown today, shots fired. One of the vics is at Detroit Receiving."

"*Lots* of shots fired. Brass all over the street."

"That's the one."

"Should I ask why you care?"

"You could."

"I won't bother. Can't tell you much. Terrence caught it."

"Haney? That's like no one catching it at all."

"Fat man's closing in on his twenty, taking it slow."

"He never took it any other way. I'd still like to know what he gets on this, though. Think you could put eyes on it?"

"If it's worth it."

"You're cheapening our friendship."

"Times are tough, brother."

"Say one hundred flat fee for whatever you give me. Another hundred for copies of the actual reports when they're in. Anything above and beyond that, we'll talk."

"Now I'm curious. Why shell out that kind of coin for 411 on a punk-ass wild west with no fatalities, no charges, and no complaints?"

"I have my reasons."

"I'm sure you do," Rico said. "I'll let you know what I find out."

He took the bottle into the house with him, locked the metal front door gate, then the door itself. The town house smelled of stale food and cigarette smoke.

He sat on the couch, pushed aside the day-old Chinese

food containers on the coffee table, and put up his feet. He loosened his tie, lit a Newport, looked at his reflection in the blank TV screen across the room. A clock ticked somewhere in the house.

It had been months since he'd done anything for Marquis. He'd gotten by in the meantime with some debt collection for local shys, a couple repo jobs in neighborhoods the professionals wouldn't go to. But it wasn't enough. The town house was paid off, but he'd had to cash in all his Treasury bonds, sell the twenty-foot Chris-Craft he'd kept out at the riverfront marina.

He'd lost his monthly pension from Detroit PD when the city had gone bankrupt. With the little he had coming in, and what he'd been dropping in the casinos, here and in Vegas, the math didn't work. He had less than twenty grand in the bank, another five in emergency cash hidden in the house.

A year back, Marquis had offered him a kilo to put on the street, let him make points on the package. Burke had turned him down. Marquis didn't want a partner, he wanted an employee. And Burke would starve before he let that happen.

He sipped bourbon, let the Newport ash grow long before he tipped it into the fried-rice carton. His buzz was back now. He took out the envelope with the ten thousand, thumbed through the bills, counting it for the first time. It was all there. He tossed it on the table, looked at it. It was a start.

There was nothing more left for him here. It was time to move on. But he'd need money for that, a lot more than what he had. And maybe now, finally, he saw a way to get it.

He listened to the empty house, the ticking clock, thought

about turning on the TV, finding a game to watch, maybe a movie. But he couldn't raise the energy. These days, he ended up sleeping on the couch more often than not anyway, too drunk to make it up to the bedroom.

When he raised the bottle again, he was surprised to see it was almost empty. He drank the last of it, turned the bottle over in his hand, angry at himself for not buying a second one when he had the chance.

He threw the bottle at the dark TV, missed. It broke against the wall.

TEN

Crissa unlocked the front door, pushed it open with her fingertips, and listened. The house was silent.

She stepped in. To her left, the alarm on the wall began to beep. She punched in the code to deactivate it, closed the door behind her.

She'd left the suitcases in the car, wanted her hands free. She walked the empty rooms, found no signs anyone had been there. The .32 was still in its holster, clipped beneath the bed.

She brought in the two suitcases, one of them full of money, locked the front door, left them in the living room. The sliding glass door that led onto the back deck was locked and barred, as she'd left it. She pulled back the vertical blinds, opened the door. The motion detector above her clicked on, bathed the deck in light.

A chill breeze blew in off the inlet. She drew up one of

the wrought-iron porch chairs, sat. The security light lit up the sloping backyard all the way to the small dock beyond. In the distance, she could see taillights on the drawbridge that linked Avon and Belmar. Looking east, toward the ocean, the far-off lights of fishing boats on the horizon. She heard the soft clang of a buoy out in the channel, the squawk of invisible seagulls overhead. The sounds of home.

She'd bought the house the year before, put down a hundred thousand dollars in cash, a fifth of the purchase price. She could have paid it off all at once, but that would have been a red flag to the IRS. On paper, she lived off low-level but steady investments—strip malls in Arkansas and Alabama, a car wash in Tennessee. They gave her cover for the life she lived, let her layer her take-home cash into legitimate sources of income. Rathka, the lawyer in New York, had set it all up for her. In the three years since she'd lost everything, had her identity compromised, forfeited all she owned, she'd built a new life.

The light clicked off, and she sat there in darkness. Her right arm and shoulder were stiff, but the pain had dulled to an arthritic ache. She'd open a bottle of wine, pop a couple of Aleve, turn on the radio to WQXR, the classical station out of New York. A long hot shower and then sleep. Tomorrow, she'd unpack the money, separate Larry's eighty thousand, stow some more in safe deposit boxes she kept at two local banks. She'd call Rathka tomorrow, decide what to do with the rest.

After a while, she went back inside, locked the door behind

her. In the bedroom, she took the .32 from its holster and checked to make sure the magazine was full, with a round in the chamber. It was a nervous habit, but she couldn't sleep otherwise. For the past few months, she'd had a recurring nightmare of a figure coming at her fast out of darkness while she pulled the trigger of an empty pistol again and again.

But those were just dreams. She fit the gun back into its holster. She was home now, safe. Alive. This time.

"You're back," Jimmy Peaches said.

She sat beside him on the bench, looked out at the empty beach, the ocean beyond.

"For a little while," she said, and set the white and gold box of cigars between them.

"Portofinos again," he said. "You're spoiling me."

"Life's too short to smoke bad cigars. Isn't that what you always say?"

Twenty feet up the boardwalk, out of earshot, the aide who'd brought him out was smoking a cigarette and talking on a cell phone. He'd nodded when he saw her approach, then wandered away.

"You pay him for that?" she said. "To mind his own business?"

"Julio's a good kid. He looks after me."

"And you take care of him as well, I'd guess."

"The little they make here, I'm happy to help out. And he looks up to me for some reason."

"Because you're an OG?"

"Me? I'm just an old man with bad legs and not much time. He feels sorry for me, more likely."

Gulls wheeled overhead. The ocean was calm and still, only a faint breeze moving the dune grass. Behind them, the retirement home cast a shadow across the boardwalk. Twenty stories of pink concrete rising into the sky, the tallest building on this side of Asbury Park.

She nodded at the red aluminum walker beside the bench. "You lost the wheelchair."

"Finally. Been a few weeks now. Can't go very far, and I'm exhausted when I get there, but it's better than being stuck in that chair, having to call someone every time I need to take a piss. Excuse my French."

He had color in his cheeks, had gained weight since the last time she'd seen him. He wore a yellow monogrammed shirt, dark slacks, black shoes polished to a mirror shine. But his hair was thinner, pink scalp showing through.

"You look good," she said.

"You're lying, but that's fine. I don't mind."

She touched the cigar box. "You want me to open these for you?"

"Not a bad idea, as long as we're out here. Might as well take advantage."

She got out her penknife, sliced through the plastic wrap and seal. "How's your grandson, Anthony?"

"He makes it down here when he can. He's got the restaurant, so he's busy with that. I think he's getting back together with the ex, too. Or trying to. I don't think he knows what he wants."

"Why do you say that?"

"Because he's always asking about you."

She closed the knife, put it away. "The kids will make the difference. He won't want to take the chance on losing them again."

"I hope not," he said. Inside the box, the cigars were in thin aluminum tubes. He took one out. "The older I get, the more I realize there's nothing more important than family."

"I'm sure you're right." She looked away.

"I'm sorry," he said after a moment. "Forgive me. I'm an old man. I forget sometimes."

"It's all right. Things are what they are. Hopefully some-day they'll be different."

"They will. What do you hear from our friend in Texas?"

"Nothing new. And I'm not expecting much anytime soon."

"It's too bad, what happened down there."

"He called the play," she said.

"Way you told it, he had his reasons."

"Maybe. But they didn't make much sense to me."

He unscrewed the tube, slid out the cigar, held it beneath his nose, inhaled. "Been a while since I had one of these. You mind?"

"Go ahead."

He leaned to one side, took a gold cigar clipper from his pants pocket.

"You're prepared," she said.

"I try to be. My age, you take your pleasures where you can."

He sliced the tip from the cigar, flicked it away, put the clipper back, got a silver lighter from the same pocket. She took it from him, opened it and thumbed the wheel. He leaned forward as she cupped her hands against the wind. He got the cigar lit, puffed. "Thank you."

He sat back, drew in smoke, held it for a moment, then let it drift back out. *"Bellissimo. Grazie."* She set the lighter atop the box.

"It's none of my business what you do," he said. "But these days I worry when I don't hear from you for a while."

"No need."

"I do, though. How did things go this time?"

"Not good."

"Not worth it?"

"The money end was fine. Too much drama getting it, though."

"What kind of drama?"

"The worst kind."

"Law?"

She shook her head.

"Someone got greedy," he said.

"Amateurs. One of them was on the string. He had a part-ner we didn't know about. Work went fine. They made their play during the count. The partner was holed up in the house we were using. We walked right into it."

"You get hurt?"

"No."

"What happened?"

"It was a four-man string. I knew two of them, had worked with them before. They both went down. I got out of there with my split, but it was a close thing."

"Then I was right to be worried. Any fallout? Anything you need to worry about going forward?"

"I don't think so. I think it's over."

"I see." He looked out over the water.

"Go on," she said. "Say it."

"Say what?"

"Whatever it is you're going to say."

He shrugged. "I'm an old man, lives in a home. Who cares what I think? All my life I minded my own business. Why stop now?"

"I respect you, Jimmy. You know that. If there's something you want to say to me, you should say it."

He puffed on the cigar, not looking at her. "That thing with Benny Roth. The money from the airport job. That went well, didn't it?"

"Yes."

"Biggest take-home in a while?"

"Ever."

"Then why'd you go out again so soon?"

She watched plovers walking along the wave line, pecking at the sand. A gull landed, chased them away, flew off with something in its beak.

"Like I said." He let out smoke. "None of my business."

"It's not that. I'm just not sure what the answer is."

"You have a home now. A real one. Some money put away, too, I'd think. And more set aside for emergencies."

"I do." Along with bank accounts and investments, she had cash in safe deposit boxes up and down the East Coast, under different names.

"Then why take unnecessary risks? Why do the work when you don't need the money?"

"You can't always control it," she said. "Sometimes it comes up when you don't need it. Other times, you need it bad, it's nowhere to be found. You have to take it as it comes."

"You believe that?"

She took out her sunglasses. "I don't know."

"The money's supposed to be a means to an end, not the end itself. You keep doing it just to do it—whether you need to or not—it'll go bad. I've seen it happen. Unless you're telling me you're in it for the thrill, happy to stick a gun in some liquor store clerk's face, clean out the register."

She shook her head.

"Then what?" he said.

"Best I can put it is, early on, I never had much of anything. Always on the move, ripping and running. Bad days. Wayne changed all that. Then suddenly I was on my own again, had to start over without him. So I built something new, worked hard at it. And then I lost it all."

"I remember."

"I had to start from scratch. And there's no telling when that could happen again. A couple bad breaks in a row, I could end up back where I was, with nothing. I need to earn while I can, enough to keep me going if things go bad."

"There's no score worth dying for."

"I know that."

"You should be on an island somewhere, someplace warm, spending your money slowly. Enjoying life before it's too late. That's what I should have done. Too many years, all I was focused on was the next dollar. I look back now, I realize how foolish I was."

"You did what you had to do."

"That's what I told myself back then, yeah. But now I see the big picture. You can always go out and find some more money somewhere. It's time that runs out. And you can't get it back."

"I know."

"Tell me, though, this other thing. You sure it's over?"

"For now. Though it's hard to accept."

"How so?"

"Two men died back there. Men I trusted, who trusted me. And a couple of amateurs walked away with half the money."

"Nothing you can do about that now."

"I could go back there, find them. Kill them."

"But there's no percentage in that, is there?" he said.

"No, there isn't."

"Keep that in mind."

They sat in silence for a few moments, watching the water. Then he said, "Before, when I said 'You're back,' you said, 'For a little while.' What's that mean?"

"I need to make another trip soon. But it shouldn't take long."

He looked at her.

"It's not what you're thinking," she said. "Just something I need to do."

"It's not work."

"No," she said. "Just a debt I have to pay."

ELEVEN

At 10:00 A.M., Burke was parked outside a Coney Island on Eight Mile, nursing hot coffee from a white Styrofoam cup. It was chasing away the headache from the Four Roses the night before but burning a hole in his stomach.

Rico's Crown Vic pulled into the lot, backed into a spot two cars away. Burke unlocked his passenger door. Rico got in, said, "You buying breakfast?" He wore a long leather coat over a suit, had a diamond stud in his left ear, a gleaming Chopard watch on his wrist.

Burke held up his cup. "I'll go coffee. Breakfast will have to be on the taxpayers."

"Cheap motherfucker." Burke had left a pack of Newports on the dash. Rico picked it up, shook one out.

"Help yourself," Burke said.

Rico tossed the pack back on the dash, took out a lighter and got the cigarette going.

"They don't let you smoke in city cars anymore," Rico said. "You believe that shit? They fine you if maintenance smells smoke, find butts in the ashtray. If I want to light up, I have to pull over, get out. Pain in the ass in the winter. I roll up on a crime scene, first thing I do is get those smokes out."

Burke took a pint of Maker's Mark from his coat pocket, said, "Here, hit this. Still your brand, right?"

"Little early in the day for that shit, isn't it?"

Burke started to put it back, and Rico said, "Hold up. Give it here."

Burke handed it over. "What you got for me?"

Rico unscrewed the cap. "What you got for *me*?" He drank from the bottle.

Burke took a white business envelope from his pocket, put it on the dash alongside the cigarettes. "Two hundred in there. For starters."

Rico put the cap back on, slipped the bottle in his pocket. "Man, you are eager, aren't you?"

"Eager enough."

Rico picked up the envelope and looked inside, thumbed bills.

"Like I said, it's a start," Burke said.

"Much appreciated." Rico slipped the envelope into an inside coat pocket. From another, he took a narrow spiral notebook with a brown cover. "Few things for you. Not a lot yet."

"Let's hear it." Burke set his coffee on the dash, got out a cigarette.

"Terrence ain't been in yet today. Had a doctor's appointment or something. Left his business all over the place, though, as usual."

"Affirmative Action at its best." Burke lit the cigarette.

"Hey, I can say that shit. You can't." Rico opened the notebook. "I wrote down what I could. He ran plates on all the vehicles at the scene. Or had someone do it for him. He got that far at least."

"How many vehicles involved?"

"Three at the scene. An SUV, a Chevy pickup, and a VW Jetta. There was a collision between the truck and the SUV. No one stuck around to exchange information. Brother popping off with an AK might have had something to do with that."

"Willie Freeman," Burke said.

"So you know some of this already."

"Just a little."

"Who is he? Who's he work for?"

"No idea. Just heard the name."

"Expect me to belicve that?"

"What about the vehicles?"

"The pickup, a Silverado, was stolen two days ago from Royal Oak. The SUV, an Armada, is registered to a grandmother in Westside who's seventy years old. Doubt she gets much use out of it."

"No surprise there. What about the Jetta?"

"Same deal. Registered to a Geraldo Rivera in Highland Park."

"Geraldo Rivera? No shit. You call his network?"

"Would have. Except this one's twenty-two years old, and his address is bogus, as in no such."

"I heard there were weapons left behind," Burke said.

"A shottie and two handguns in the Armada, plus the AK our man Willie was waving around. Serial numbers on all of them. I guess Terrence'll run them when he gets around to it. AK was the only one fired."

"And how's Mr. Freeman?"

"He's still at Detroit Receiving. GSW to hip and shoulder. Had surgery last night. He'll live, but he isn't saying much."

"He have a sheet?"

"Nothing major. Possession with intent. A couple weapons beefs. No serious time."

"What'd he tell Terrence?"

"Same old. Shot by unidentified assailants in a drive-by. Don't know who. Don't know why. Says one of them dropped the AK, he picked it up, returned fire. Says he doesn't know anything about the Armada, it was parked there when he came walking along. But I'm betting his fingerprints are all over it."

"A stand-up guy. I may need to talk to him."

"Terrence didn't get much, and he was holding a gun charge over him for the AK. What makes you think he'll talk to you?"

"My personality. He the only one got dropped?"

"On scene, at least. Nothing from any hospitals. If one of the other shooters got hit, his homies took him with them."

"What kind of brass on the ground?"

"Seven-six-two casings, from the AK. Some 5.56 from another rifle."

"AR-15," Burke said.

"Maybe. Shotgun shells, too, 12-gauge buck and deer slugs."

"They came to play."

"Not to mention the smoke grenades. But maybe you heard about that, too?"

Burke smiled, sipped coffee. "Like I said. Just a little."

"All I got right now. I'll holler at you if I find out anything else. You want me to talk to Terrence?"

"No. Better off without him, I think."

"Let me get one of those butts for later."

"Take the pack. How are things at Beaubien Street these days?"

"Lots of empty desks," Rico said. "Phones ringing, nobody answering. Last round of early outs hurt us bad. You miss the job?"

"Not for a minute."

"You been doing okay, though, ain't you? Out there on your own."

"I get by."

"You still do work for Marquis?"

"Now and then. Not much lately."

"Never liked that motherfucker."

"You took his money, too, back in the day."

"When I had to."

"No one put a gun to your head. And look at it this way, people will always do dope. And somebody will always be around to sell it to them. Better Marquis than some other asshole leaving bodies everywhere."

"Marquis's left his share. But let me ask you this. Why is this lame-ass drive-by giving you such a hard-on? What's the interest?"

"Violence against my city is violence against me."

Rico gave a short laugh. "Ever a time you actually felt that way?"

"First day on the job. For two hours, maybe. Maybe three."

"That long?"

"Couldn't help it," Burke said. "I'm a romantic."

When Burke got off the elevator, there was a uniformed patrolman leaning against the counter at the nurses' station. Young black guy, but already overweight, a roll of fat spilling over his belt. He nodded at Burke, cocked his head down the hall.

Burke went past, the uni following him. When they were out of sight of the nurses, Burke said, "Darius, right? Don't think we've met. How you doing?"

"Doing a'right." Thumbs in his belt, waiting.

At the far end of the hall, a door was ajar, a yellow plastic chair outside.

"That him?" Burke said.

Darius nodded. Burke took out a folded fifty-dollar bill, held it waist high between two fingers.

Darius looked at it. "Rico said a hundred."

"Did he?"

"Could lose my job over this."

"You got nothing to worry about." Leaving the bill out there. Darius shook his head.

Burke got out another fifty, folded it over the first. Darius took the money, put it in his shirt pocket. "How much time you need?"

"Twenty minutes," Burke said. "Half hour at most. Need some privacy, though."

"Can't be no trouble."

"Won't be."

Darius looked down to the nurses' station, then back at him. "You used to be on the job, huh?"

"I was."

"Half hour?"

"Tops."

Darius nodded, went back down the hall.

It was a private room. A black man with patches of gray in his hair was propped up in the bed, right arm in a sling. He was watching a TV mounted high on the wall.

Burke closed the door behind him, said, "Willie Freeman. Just the man I'm looking for."

Freeman turned to look at him. "Who are you?" He had monitor wires running inside his hospital gown, an IV tube in his left wrist.

"You're looking pretty good for a man just got shot," Burke said. "How you feeling?"

"I already talked to a detective."

"I know. Lieutenant Haney, right? Funny, everybody thinks I look like a cop. Why is that?"

"What you want?" His gown was loose, and Burke could see the bulk of the bandage on his right shoulder.

"My name's Frank Burke." He pulled a plastic chair closer to the bed, sat. "That mean anything to you?"

"Should it?" He looked toward the door.

"He's not out there," Burke said. "He's taking a break." He looked up at the screen. "What are you watching there? *Sanford and Son* reruns?"

"I asked what you want."

"You're older than most of Marquis's boys. Must mean you're higher on the food chain, right? How's the shoulder? You right-handed?"

Freeman watched him, didn't answer.

"I got shot once," Burke said. "In the stomach. It was back in '91, when shit was going crazy here with all the crack. I was lucky, it was just a .22. Cheap street gun. Still hurt like a mother, though. Guy who shot me was named Baby-Boy Roberts. You ever hear of him?"

Freeman shook his head.

"Worked for the Chambers Brothers," Burke said. "Actually, he worked for somebody worked for the Chambers Brothers. I'm sure they had no idea who he was."

"Don't know the man."

"It was a straight buy-and-bust, undercover. When Baby-Boy saw what the deal was, he pulled out this piece-of-shit revolver, goddamn thing held together by electrician's tape, and started blasting. He got me with the first one, the next two missed. Couldn't shoot for shit, lucky for me."

"Yeah?"

"Yeah. Then I put a .38 steel jacket in his left eye, blew the back of his head all over a brick wall."

"Why you telling me this?"

"So we get to know each other a little. Find our common ground."

"Man, I don't know who the fuck you are. And I got nothing to say to you."

Burke took out his cell, tossed it on the bed. "I got Marquis on speed dial. You want to talk to him?"

Freeman looked at the phone.

"Who do you think gave me your name, dickwag?" Burke said. "Stop wasting my time."

"I don't know what you talking about."

"You talk to Damien already? He been by here?"

"Damien who?"

Burke picked up the phone, put it back in his pocket. Freeman looked back up at the screen. Burke reached over, took the television remote from his lap.

"Hey, what you doing—"

Burke found the button, and the screen went dark. "I need your undivided attention here, Willie, or we're going to get off on the wrong foot."

He put the remote on the bedside stand, out of Freeman's reach. "I'll ask again. Damien been here?"

"Who's that?"

"Careful how you play this, Willie. I admire you. You're a good man. Loyal. Hell, Marquis should give you a bonus for catching those hot ones, being the only one with the balls to grab some iron, return fire."

He looked at Freeman's IV setup, two clear bags hanging from a J-shaped pole above the monitor.

"What they got you on? Demerol drip? Antibiotics, too, right? Good shit, Demerol. You'll need a lot of it in the next couple weeks. Private doctor, too, and a physical therapist. Not to mention a lawyer. Marquis gonna pay for all that?"

"I don't need any lawyer."

"You will. I've got friends at Beaubien Street, and word is they're putting a charge on you for the AK. You're looking at a mandatory ten years there."

"I ain't taking no charge. *I* was the one got shot."

"Won't make any difference. You were the one with the weapon. And aside from Detroit PD, you'll have Marquis to worry about."

"Why?"

"Because it was a setup, right? Only way it makes sense. That's what I told him."

"Wasn't no setup."

He looked past Burke to the door.

"Nobody's coming in here until I let them," Burke said. "It's just you and me, William. Now, Marquis gave me a list of seven names. You, the two boys in the Armada, and four others who knew about the drop-off. Not counting Damien. You were the easiest to find, so here I am."

"I got nothing to say."

"Let me show you something. Just for the sake of argument." He leaned forward, took the leather slapjack from his back pocket. "Ever see one of these?"

Freeman looked at it.

"This thing belongs in a museum now, but when I first joined the department, all the old-timers carried these." He tapped the thick end on the bed rail, made it clang and vibrate. "Those old guys really knew how to use these, especially up close. All that lead shot sewn into the business end. Just a flick of the wrist"—he slapped it against the bed rail again, harder this time—"and they could really put the hurt on you. Crack a skull. Break an elbow or knee, no problem."

"What about it?"

"Well, we can have a civil conversation here, or it can go the other way, too. I can put a pillow over your face, start whaling on that shoulder." He nodded at the bandage. "In five seconds I'll fuck up what it took those doctors five hours to fix. You'll be jacking off with your left hand for the rest of your life."

Freeman tried to sit up straighter, his face tightened with pain.

"You know I mean it," Burke said.

"Ain't no need to talk like that." The fear in him now.

"Willie, let's get some things straight. You're a piece of shit, works for a dope dealer. We both know that. I spent twenty-five years dealing with pieces of shit like you. That was my job. So let's back up a little. You talk to Damien?"

Freeman shifted his arm in the sling. "Yeah, he was here."

"When?"

"This afternoon. Right after they moved me."

"What did you tell him?"

"I thought you said you were working for Marquis?"

"I'm not working for anyone. What did you tell him?"

"Just what I saw."

"And what was that?"

"How much you hear?"

"Enough that if you try to feed me a line of crap, I'll know it. How many of them were there?"

Freeman drew a deep breath, let it out. "Four. At least. One drove the truck that hit us. There were three more in the van. Two of them came out, did the drop car. Driver stayed inside the whole time. I never saw him."

"But you saw the others?"

"They wore masks."

"They white, black?"

"Couldn't tell."

"You're leaving something out."

Freeman looked away. Burke brought the chair closer, put the slapjack away.

"You know what Damien's doing right now?" he said. "He's talking to the others on that list, trying to find out what happened. And some of them, to save their own asses, are going to point the finger at you. Now, Damien doesn't have to worry about you. He knows where you are, that you aren't going anywhere. He'll take his time. And when he finds out what he wants, he'll be back to take care of business."

"You don't know that."

"But I do. Now tell me, when all that lead was flying, you hit anyone?"

He inched higher in the bed. "Just one."

"Kill him?"

"I thought so, at first, 'cause it was a clean shot, and she went down fast. But the other two helped her into the van. Looked like she was moving okay by then."

"She?"

"Yeah, I think."

"What's that mean, you 'think'?"

"From the shape of her, way she ran, I'd say a woman."

"Try again."

"You asked me what I saw."

Burke frowned. "That's some sad bullshit you're trying to put over on me." He took the slapjack from his pocket again.

"Hold up. That's no bullshit."

"You tell Damien this?"

Freeman nodded.

"Let me ask you," Burke said. "How many women you know in D-Town, gangsta bitches, run with a slick crew like that?"

"Man, I don't know."

"How about none?" He rested the slapjack on his leg. "What did those boys with you see?"

"They didn't see shit. That truck came out of nowhere, knocked us all on our asses. Then came the smoke, someone popping caps outside. Those boys stayed on the floor the whole time. After I went down, they piled out of there, hauled ass. Left all their shit behind."

"Left you behind, too. How much money was in the Jetta?"

"Not my business what was in there."

He put the slapjack away, thought it through. Damien already one step ahead of him. Marquis playing them against each other, waiting to see who got to the money first. Smart.

"The crew that took you down knew too much," Burke said. "Odds are someone on that list gave it up. That's what Marquis will think, true or not. Maybe he'll decide it was you."

"Don't say shit like that."

"It's the truth, Willie. This train's rolling. You want to get out in front of it, or run over and dragged behind? Your choice."

"Marquis and I go back a long way."

"Doesn't matter. This is business. He'll whack all of you just to be sure. You'll end up in a vacant on the East Side, two in the head, courtesy of his brother. Even if you're in County, waiting trial, he'll get to you. Have someone throw your ass over the tier with an extension cord around your neck. You know I'm right."

Freeman shook his head, looked away.

"Here's my advice," Burke said. "Get out of Detroit. Soon as you can. Jump bail if you have to, whatever. Just get away. Even if he doesn't find out who took his money, Marquis will tie up the loose ends, make an example out of all of you."

"What you want from me?"

Burke took the calfskin card holder from his inside pocket,

slipped out a card. It read INVESTIGATIONS, CORPORATE/ PERSONAL, and in smaller type, FRANCIS X. BURKE. No phone number or address. He turned it over, took out a silver pen, wrote his cell number on the back.

"Might be you could save me some time," he said. "Take the heat off yourself as well. And there's money in it for you."

"What money?"

"Money I'd give you. Running money. Enough to get away somewhere, get clear. I can help you do that, too. I know a lot of people."

Burke dropped the card in his lap.

"Somebody on the inside made this happen," he said. "Somebody you know. You remember anything else—a name, a conversation, anything—you call me. Not Marquis, not Damien. Just me. Do that and I might be able to keep you alive. With some cash for your trouble as well."

"How much?"

"Give me a name—one that pays off—and we'll talk about it."

"I'm supposed to trust you now?"

"Willie, I'm the only one you *can* trust. Marquis won't sit still for someone taking his money. Or somebody else standing by letting it happen. Stay around here and you're a dead man."

Freeman picked up the card.

"This right now," Burke said, "is where this life led you. There's no going back to the way things were. You need to accept that."

He took two fifties from his coat pocket, tucked them in Freeman's sling.

"A name, that's all I need. Think about it, Willie. And do the smart thing."

TWELVE

Pinned to the front door was a red sheet of paper that said, in large black type, FORECLOSURE NOTICE. Paragraphs of smaller print, then at the bottom, in the same black font, KEEP OUT.

Crissa rang the doorbell, listened to it sound inside. The house was yellow stucco, the paint sun-faded, the yard full of weeds. Through a gap in the front blinds, she could see a bare floor littered with trash—fast-food containers, cigarette butts, a naked Barbie doll with one arm missing. She tried the door. Locked.

She'd taken Amtrak from Metro Park to Philadelphia, changed there for the train to Orlando. An hour to Philly, and another twenty to Florida. She'd slept fitfully in her seat, waking every few hours. Leaving the train that morning, she'd carried two suitcases, one with clothes, the other with eighty thousand dollars in banded cash.

A taxi had taken her to a hotel near the airport. There she'd rented a Ford Fusion for the half-hour drive north to Winter Park, found the address she'd gotten from an Internet database. It was a neighborhood of single-story crackerbox houses with missing shingles, dead lawns, and ten-year-old cars.

She rang the bell again, then went around to the backyard. Wind-blown trash, yellow weeds, dog droppings. The back windows and door were plywooded over. She felt a vague depression settling over her. She knew neighborhoods like this, had lived in them.

"That's private property."

She heard a screen door open, turned to see a woman come out onto the back porch of the neighboring house. She was in her sixties, stringy gray hair brushed back, holding a faded housecoat closed with one hand. A small dog barked behind her. She pushed it back inside, closed the screen. The barking kept on, a flat yapping with long pauses in between.

Crissa took off her sunglasses, hung them from the collar of her T-shirt, said, "Hi, maybe you can help me. I'm looking for the family that lived here."

The woman said, "Josephine, hush up," and the dog growled low, then went quiet. "There's nobody there now."

"I can see that," Crissa said. "How long have they been gone?"

The woman stepped down into the yard. "Are you from the bank?"

"No, just a friend of the family."

"And you didn't know they were gone?"

"I didn't."

"Sheriff's office put them out. They had some furniture and things, went out on the lawn. It all got picked over. Bunch of vultures around here."

"They were evicted?" Crissa said.

"Took long enough. It's a shame what was going on there."

"What do you mean?"

"You say you know the family?"

Crissa took a breath, deciding how to play it, what to say next.

"I'm a friend of Larry Black's. This was his house, right?" Smiling, wanting to keep the woman talking.

"Larry hasn't been around here in a long time."

"I know."

"And I don't remember ever seeing you here before."

"He and I used to work together, up north. What did you mean by 'what was going on' here?"

"This used to be a good neighborhood. Now look at it. Nobody takes care of their property. Half the houses are vacant, yards are a mess. I called the Code Enforcement twice this month, lot of good it did me. They don't care. They just want us all out of here, so they can take the lots, sell them to a developer."

"Things that bad around here?" Not pushing it, letting the woman tell it her way.

"When Larry lived there, it was different. He'd look after things, do work for me, too, if I needed it. But once he was gone . . . well, it's a sin what happened. People coming and going all night long, motorcycles and loud cars. Parties, fights. I had to call the police a few times myself. And that little girl there the whole time, too."

"Haley?" Crissa said.

"That's the worst part. That child in the middle of it all. As many times as the police were here, I'm surprised Social Services didn't take her. She'd be better off."

"It's Haley I'm looking for. Do you have any idea where they went?"

"That motel up by the highway, I'd guess. Same place most go when they get evicted around here, if they don't have family. They can't come back here. Bank's got the house, changed the locks."

"How long ago did they leave?"

"Two weeks maybe. At least. Is Larry coming back?"

"No," Crissa said. "He isn't."

"That's too bad. He's a good man. Deserved better than he got with that Claudette."

The name would make it easier to find her. The house had been listed under Larry's name alone.

"You come a long way, haven't you?" the woman said.

Crissa blinked, said, "What?"

"To get here. You look exhausted. You come down from up north?"

"I did."

"Why are you looking for Haley?"

"I have something to give her."

"From her father?"

"Yes."

"If you see him when you get back, you tell him Enid next door says hello. He'll know who I am."

"All right."

"And tell him we miss him around here."

"I will," Crissa said. "When I see him again."

The Islander Inn was two stories of faded paint and dirty windows, with an old-style neon sign in the shape of a palm tree. A marquee below it read COLOR TV, PHONES and YOUR HOME AWAY FROM HOME. On one side of the motel was a shuttered Sunoco station. On the other, a half-empty strip mall.

She pulled into the motel lot, backed into a space. There was a fenced-in pool area to one side, but the pool was empty, the concrete cracked. Stone planters lined the street side, full of weeds and cigarette butts. On the corner, a bearded man stood facing the street, holding a cardboard sign that read, in black marker, HOMELESS VET. WILL WORK FOR FOOD. GOD BLESS THE USA. A dog lay curled at his feet.

It had rained on the short drive here, a downpour that ended almost as soon as it had begun. The sun was out again now, steam rising off the blacktop. To the west, a rainbow arced across the sky. She shut off the engine, and the windshield almost immediately began to fog.

The motel was L-shaped, maybe thirty rooms, most of those with drapes closed tight. Half a dozen cars in the lot, including a dented Volvo with plastic sheeting where the passenger window used to be. A shiny pickup with a jacked-up frame and a bumper sticker that read EVERYTHING I NEED TO KNOW ABOUT ISLAM I LEARNED ON 9/11.

Through the door marked OFFICE, she could see a small lobby, a bulletproof window where the desk clerk would be. No one behind it now. She felt the depression again. She'd lived in places like this, too.

Two Hispanic men sat on the concrete staircase, smoking cigarettes, They were in their twenties, wore cheap T-shirts with faded logos, jeans, and work boots. An emaciated woman in cutoffs and tank top came out of a first-floor room and stood out on the sidewalk, cell phone to her ear. The men watched her.

She looked over at Crissa without taking the phone away, then went back to her conversation. A few minutes later, a car pulled into the entrance. She leaned in through the open passenger window, spoke to the driver, took a last look back at Crissa, then got in. The car pulled back out.

You look like a cop parked here, Crissa thought. You're making everybody nervous.

She got out of the car, the air thick with humidity. The men watched her as she approached.

"*Hola,*" she said. "*Estoy buscando una mujer que vive aquí, con un niño pequeño, una niña.*" Telling them she was looking for a woman living there with a little girl.

The men looked at each other, then back at her. The one on the right, in a Kenny Chesney T-shirt, said, "*Policía?*"

"*No,*" she said. She rested a boot on the bottom step. "*Servicios Sociales. Niños y Familias.*"

The one in the Kenny Chesney shirt scaled his cigarette onto the wet blacktop. "I speak English. My name's Eduardo."

"The little girl, she's about six. She and her mother live here, I think. Last name is Black. That sound like anyone around here?"

The one on the left, still smoking, said, *"Adictos a las drogas."*

She looked at him. "What?"

"Metanfetamina," Eduardo said. "Tweakers."

"Sí," the smoker said.

"I'd appreciate if you could help me," she said. Then, so they both understood, *"Estaría en su deuda."*

She took a ten from her jeans pocket, held it out. The smoker looked at it, said, *"Diez dólares. No es mucho."* Wanting more.

"Veinte," she said. *"Diez para cada uno de ustedes. Eso es todo lo que tengo."* She took out another ten, folded the two together.

"Treinta," the smoker said, but Eduardo frowned, waved that off. He cocked his head toward the second floor. "I think the people you want, they're in 216. The father lives there, too."

"Father?"

"Maybe her father. Maybe not. *El cabrón.* A bad guy."

She looked up at the second floor. Two-sixteen was on the short end of the L, facing the parking lot.

"This isn't a place for *niños*," Eduardo said. "You'd do that little girl a favor, you take her away from here."

She set the money on the step between them, said, *"Gra-cias."* They moved apart to let her pass.

She walked down the balcony to 216, aware the two were watching her. The heavy drapes were drawn over the window. She listened at the door, heard a TV on inside. She knocked. When there was no answer, she put her ear closer to the door. Music and sound effects. Cartoons.

She knocked again, said, "Haley?" and listened. No response.

She took out the pocket notebook and pen she'd brought. *Claudette,* she wrote, *I'm a friend of Larry's. We need to talk. Call me,* and added her cell number.

She tore the page from the notebook, slid it under the door so only a single white corner showed. Then she backed away to the railing, waited. A movement in the curtain, then it was still again. If Haley's in there alone, she probably won't open the door, Crissa thought. And that's a good thing.

The triangle of paper disappeared.

She waited two more minutes, in case anyone inside wanted another look at her, but the drapes were still.

She went back down the stairs, between the two men. *"Gra-cias,"* she said again as she passed.

"Por nada," Eduardo said.

When she was almost at the car, he said, "Hey."

She turned, looked back.

"If you come back, be careful," he said. "Especially at night. There are bad people here. It's not safe."

"I'll keep that in mind," she said.

* * *

Back at the hotel, she showered, had dinner in the restaurant, drank a second glass of wine after the waitress cleared the table. Through the big window, she watched the sun set, the clouds turn violet.

On the table, her phone began to buzz. A 407 area code. When she answered, a woman said, "Who is this?"

"Claudette?"

"Who are you?"

"I'm a friend of Larry's."

"I saw your note. What do you want?"

"If this is Claudette, then you know what I'm talking about. We should meet. I may have something for you. But we have to talk first."

"Talk about what?"

"Better we do it in person."

"Come to think of it, I don't know any Larry after all. Don't come by here again."

"Don't hang up," Crissa said. "You're being careful, I understand. I used to work with him."

Silence on the line. Then, "Where?"

"Different places. With mutual friends. Detroit. Houston." Leaving that last one out there, wondering if it meant anything to her, if she knew what had happened there.

"What's your name?" the woman said.

"When we talk. Tomorrow."

"You say you've got something for me?"

"Maybe."

"What's that mean?"

"When we talk."

Another silence. The woman thinking it over, the hook set.

"You know where I am," she said finally. "Bring what you got," and ended the call.

THIRTEEN

The woman who opened the door had been pretty once. Midthirties, blond hair cut short. But she was too skinny, the black T-shirt hanging loose around her, Crissa remembering then what the two men had told her. She wore low-rise jeans, two inches of skin showing between pants and T-shirt, a pale scar where a navel ring had been.

Crissa looked past her. Two-sixteen was an efficiency, a small living room with pullout couch, club chair, bureau, and TV. A short hallway that led to a kitchenette. A closed door on either side, bedroom and bathroom, she guessed. She could smell stale fried food, and a faint chemical odor she couldn't place.

"Claudette?"

The woman kept one hand on the door, ready to close it again. "I never got your name."

"Crissa."

"Crissa what?"

"Can I come in?"

The woman looked past her, along the balcony, then at the lot below.

"I'm alone," Crissa said.

The woman looked at her, then held the door open wider. She went in.

"Claudette Black?"

The woman nodded, fished a bent pack of Marlboros and a cheap plastic lighter from a jeans pocket, got one out. "How'd you find me?"

"It wasn't hard."

She lit the cigarette. Crissa looked around. There was a talk show on the TV, the sound turned down. On the bureau alongside the set was a scuffed DVD player, a handful of disc cases, knockoff DVDs with faded black-and-white inserts. The first ones were animated children's films. The last two were porn discs.

"What did you bring?" Claudette said.

"Nothing, this time." She looked around. "Is Haley here?"

"Larry never mentioned anyone named Crissa."

"He wouldn't."

"He told you about Haley?"

"A little."

"He's dead, isn't he?"

Crissa didn't answer.

The woman blew out smoke, turned to the hall. "Haley!"

When there was no answer, she said to Crissa, "She's not good with strangers." Then, louder, "Haley, get out here. Now!"

One of the doors opened, and a little girl came out. She kept her eyes on the floor. Her long dark hair was matted and dull, with a single blue plastic barrette on one side. She wore jeans and a pink Minnie Mouse T-shirt, yellow sneakers with blue flowers. She had a yellow earbud in each ear, held a pink iPod tightly in her hand.

"Come here," Claudette said. "I want you to meet someone."

"Hello," Crissa said, and when the girl looked up at her, she saw Larry's pale blue eyes. Something tugged inside her.

"How are you, Haley?" She held out her hand. "My name's Crissa."

The girl took a step back, looked at her mother.

"Get those things out of your ears," Claudette said. "Be polite."

Haley took out the earbuds, carefully wound the thin cord around the iPod, looked at the floor again.

Crissa crouched, hands on her thighs. "What are you listening to there, Haley?"

"My songs." She wouldn't meet her eyes.

"What songs?"

"My sing-alongs."

"Can I see?"

She reached for the iPod, but Haley took another step back, said softly, "It's mine."

"I know it is. I'm not going to keep it."

"Go on, Haley," Claudette said. "Don't be a little bitch."

Crissa looked at her. "What did you say?"

"She has to learn."

Haley held out the iPod. Crissa took it, saw the front casing was cracked, the screen blank, knew from its lightness there was no battery inside.

"Where did you get this?"

"From Daddy's friend. He said I could keep it."

"Then you better hang on to it." She handed it back, brushed a strand of hair from the girl's eyes. "What's yours is yours, honey. No one's going to take it away from you."

She looked at Claudette. "Let's talk outside."

They went out on the balcony. Crissa rested her elbows on the railing, looked down at the lot below, took a breath, trying to hold down her anger. This is none of your business, she thought. It never was.

Claudette came up beside her. "What is it you've got for me?"

A boy and girl, maybe seven or eight, were chasing each other around the fenced-in pool area, laughing. The sun was high and bright, but there were gray clouds to the west, darkening the horizon.

Crissa let out her breath slow, turned. "At the moment, I'm thinking I don't have anything for you at all."

"What's that mean?" She rubbed a scab on her arm.

"Haley live here with you?"

"Of course, she's my daughter."

"Who else?"

"Lives here? What's it to you?"

"I'm about to walk away from here," Crissa said. "And you're never going to see me again. That what you want?"

"What I want is for you to tell me what Larry gave you."

"Why isn't she in school?"

"School?"

"Yeah, school. Girl her age should be in school, not sitting in a motel room all day alone."

"You telling me how to raise my daughter?"

Crissa shook her head, looked away again. Don't get into it with her, she thought. It'll be a waste of time.

"How do I even know you're who you say?" Claudette said. "For all I know, you're a cop. When did you see Larry last?"

"A few days ago."

"You worked together?"

"We did."

"What kind of work?"

"Kind of work Larry sometimes did." Crissa looked at her.

Claudette crossed her arms, drew on the cigarette. "What happened?"

"He was involved in something. It didn't go the way it was supposed to."

"You were with him?"

"Yes."

Claudette looked away. "I knew it would happen someday. I should have guessed. I didn't get a check from him this month. Last month, either." She blew out smoke. "Way it always was with him, whole time we were together. Feast or famine. I got tired of it."

"What happened with the house?"

"What do you mean?"

"I went by there, where you used to live."

"Bank took it. Nobody cuts you a break these days, no matter what you're going through. Money's all they care about."

"You didn't pay the mortgage?"

"They said I didn't. When they told me they were going to foreclose, court order and everything, I said, 'Go ahead. You want it so bad, take it.' Goddamn thieves. They sent the sheriff to put us out."

"Larry was sending you money regular?" Tires screeched as a car pulled out below.

"Some. Not enough."

"What were you doing with it?"

"Seems to me you're doing a lot of asking and not much telling. Were you sleeping with him?"

"No."

Claudette rubbed a forearm. "He ever talk about me?"

"Yes. About Haley, too."

"Haley? She was only four when we split up. He hardly knew her."

"He was still her father. What did she mean by 'Daddy's friend'?"

"That's what she calls Roy. I told her he knew her father. He didn't, but it makes it easier, you know. Helps her understand."

"Who's Roy?"

"My husband."

"Husband?"

"Practically. As soon as things settle down, we'll get all the legal stuff straightened out. What do you care anyway?"

"I don't. I just care about the girl. Was she in there when I came by yesterday?"

"We taught her not to answer the door for anyone except me and Roy. There's a lot of white trash in this place. Mexicans, too."

Crissa watched a man come in off the street. He stopped at the vending machines next to the office, checked the coin return slots.

"It was hard for me, too, you know," Claudette said. "Those years I spent with Larry. Him disappearing the way he did. Never knowing if I'd see him again. If he was dead or in jail, and if I'd ever even hear about it if he was. You get tired of living like that."

"This is better?"

"It's just until things get organized. Then maybe we can get a house again. It won't be long."

"You and Roy work?"

"We do what we can."

Crissa took a breath, said, "Here's the deal. I have some money for you, from Larry. But I have the feeling if I give it to you now, you and this Roy are going to end up dead inside a week. I don't know what it is you two are doing, but I'm betting you burn through cash quick."

"You don't know anything about us. If that money's mine, it's mine. You don't get to decide."

"Well, when you talk to this Roy—"

"You can talk to him yourself. Here he comes."

Crissa turned. The man who'd walked into the lot was coming along the balcony toward them. He stopped about twenty feet away, looked at her, trying to decide whether to keep coming or not. Wondering who she was, what he was walking into.

"Hey, babe," Claudette said.

He took that as his cue, came forward, taking his time. He was skinny, with dark hair in a ponytail, a star tattoo on his neck. Red flannel shirt buttoned to the neck and cuffs despite the heat. To hide the scabs, she guessed. As he got closer, she saw his left eye was swollen, the cheek bruised.

"What happened to you?" Claudette said.

He said, "Hey," then turned to Crissa. "Do I know you?"

She faced him. He smelled vaguely of sweat and something harsher, metallic.

"She's a friend of Larry's," Claudette said.

"What's that asshole want?"

"She's got something for us. Money."

"What money?"

"Take a step back," Crissa said.

"What?"

"You heard me."

"What if I don't?"

"Then maybe I'll throw your ass over this railing, see how you land."

She held his eyes. He backed up, looking her over, turned to Claudette, said, "What is this?"

"Larry's dead," Claudette said.

"So?"

"I made a mistake," Crissa said. "I'll see you around."

Claudette put a hand on her elbow, said, "Wait."

Crissa looked at her. She took her hand away.

Crissa looked back at Roy, then at the half-open door. It had been a mistake coming here, seeing the way they were living, seeing the girl. But now she had, and there was no going back.

She looked at Roy. "Who hit you?"

"It's nothing. It was personal."

"Personal," she said.

Claudette said, "Did you go see Blue? He do that to you?"

"I said it's nothing. Just leave it, okay?"

"Who's Blue?" Crissa said.

Claudette folded her arms, scratched her elbow. "It's a long story."

"I'm here," Crissa said. "Tell it."

They sat at a concrete table on the far side of the building, near the bottom of the stairwell closest to 216. No windows on this side of the building, and no parking. Just a Dumpster with a stained mattress leaning against it, out of sight of the rest of the rooms.

Crissa faced the parking lot, Claudette and Roy on the other side. When they were done talking, Claudette got out her cigarettes and lighter.

"Let me get one of those," Roy said, and she gave him the

pack. He poked inside it, came out with a bent cigarette, used the lighter, set it back down. Claudette picked up the pack, shook it. There was nothing left inside but loose tobacco.

"How much do you owe them?" Crissa said.

He drew on the cigarette, his foot tapping the concrete. "Enough."

"How much?"

"What's it matter?"

"Roy," Claudette said.

"Because I might be able to help you," Crissa said. "And I mean might."

"And why would you do that?" he said.

"Don't misunderstand. If I do, it'll be for that little girl. Not for either of you."

"What if we don't want your help?"

"Then I'll be on my way," she said. She stood.

"Hold on," Claudette said.

"You two are wasting my time. You need to make a decision here."

"I'm sorry," Claudette said. "We told you most of it."

Crissa sat back down, looked at Roy. "Give me a figure."

He scratched his neck. "Three thousand. Thereabouts."

"You told me it was two," Claudette said.

"It was," he said. "Then."

"How long have you been dealing for them?" Crissa said.

"Not that long," he said. "A few months."

"What kind of pills?"

"Just O-Bombs," he said. "That's it. No hard stuff."

"O-Bombs?"

"Opies," Claudette said. "Opana. Painkillers."

"The old ones are the good ones," he said. "New ones aren't as strong. But Blue and Jackson got a deep stash. People pay forty bucks a pop for those. Sometimes more."

"How many did you lose?"

"Maybe a hundred. Nothing I could do. The cops were all over this place that day, busting people for anything. I tossed the bag into one of the planters, figured I'd go back and get it after they left. But the cops found it, first thing."

"And Blue didn't believe you."

"He didn't give a shit one way or another. He just wants his money."

"What did you expect?" Crissa said.

"It wasn't my fault."

A palmetto bug landed on the table, started to crawl across, antennae waving. Claudette backed away from it. Crissa flicked it off the table with a finger.

"So what happens next?" she said.

"I don't know," he said.

Claudette said, "Tell us about the money."

"How much meth you doing?"

"What?" Claudette said.

"Meth. The two of you are crawling out of your skins. You dealing it, too?"

"No," he said. "I swear." He crossed his heart. "Just the

pills. Nothing heavy. I wouldn't do that. I wouldn't get involved in that."

"You give us the money," Claudette said, "and maybe we can settle all this. We can get out of here, too, find a different place to live. Someplace better for Haley."

Crissa sat back, crossed her arms, knowing what they were doing, using the girl against her, thinking only about that money.

"We need that cash," Claudette said. "It's mine anyway. That's what Larry wanted. That's what you told me."

"Yeah," Roy said. "If it's hers, it's hers, right?"

To Claudette, she said, "You have any other family around here?"

"Family?"

"Parents? Brothers, sisters?"

"I have a sister, but we haven't talked in a while. She and Roy don't get along."

"I'm shocked," Crissa said. "Where does she live?"

"Up in St. Augustine Beach. South of Jacksonville."

"How far's that from here?"

"Driving? Three hours, maybe four."

"But I'm betting you don't have a car, right?"

"Not at the moment," Claudette said.

"What's your sister do?"

"She's a nursing supervisor at a hospital up there."

"She's a stuck-up bitch," Roy said.

Crissa looked at him, then back at Claudette. "She married, have kids?"

"Mike, her husband, passed away last year. No kids. Why?"

"With all this going on, you might want to think about taking Haley up there for a while, wait for things to blow over."

"We don't need to do that," he said. "If I can pay off Blue, everything will be fine. Nobody has to go anywhere."

"You really believe that?" Crissa said.

"Why not?"

Crissa shook her head. "You're something, you two."

"It's not my fault," he said. "I'm just trying to provide for my family, keep it all together, you know? I caught a bad break."

Crissa looked to the west. The clouds were closer now, the color of scorched pewter. She thought of Haley upstairs, wondered if she was scared of thunder.

"So what about the money?" Claudette said.

"We'll talk about it tomorrow."

"Why are you playing me like this? This isn't right. It's my money, isn't it?"

"I'd like to come by tomorrow, take Haley out for a couple hours, if it's okay with you. Get her away from this place for a little while. When I get back, we'll talk."

"You think I'm a bad mother, is that it?"

"I didn't say that."

"You have kids?"

"What's that got to do with anything?"

"Who are you to judge me? You don't know what kind of

mother I am. I love Haley. She's all I've got in the world. And I'm all she's got."

"I know," Crissa said, and stood. "And that's the problem, isn't it?"

FOURTEEN

Burke looked up at the burned-out house. The roof had caved, and the second-floor windows showed daylight. All the first-floor windows were gone, the outer walls scorched and blackened. The air smelled of smoke, burnt plastic, and dampness. Yellow crime scene tape was strung across the front door.

"Rain kept the fire down," Rico said behind him. He was leaning against his Crown Vic, arms folded. "Would have burned to the ground otherwise."

Burke walked up the driveway, cinders crunching under his shoes. In the backyard were three burned-out cars, scared and twisted metal sitting on rims, tires melted off. A garage, open and empty, was black with smoke but intact.

Rico came up the driveway behind him. "With all those cars, fire-rescue thought there were more people in there.

Turned out to only be one. Homicide ran plates and VINs, though. Two of them were stolen, and the one on the end there"—he pointed—"is a rental."

"They get an ID on the body?"

"Not yet. They'll do dental X-rays, DNA. See if they can find a match in the system. Might take months for all that, though. ME says he was dead before the fire started. Half a dozen GSWs, at least two to the head."

Burke got out his cigarettes, lit one. "Someone covering their tracks."

"Could be. Thing is though, all the way out here, if it hadn't been for the fire, nobody might have found him at all. Fire's what called attention to it. Half the houses around here probably have bodies in them."

Burke looked around. The bushes lining the driveway were black and stubbed, but the house next door was untouched.

"Fire call came in a couple hours after that drive-by you were asking about," Rico said. "Then a Shots Fired call same night, same neighborhood. Nobody checked it out 'til the next day, though. That's when they found the other one. Two bodies, GSWs, same block. Not too hard to put that together."

"Where was the other one?"

"'Round the way."

"Show me."

They went back down the driveway to the street.

"You asked me to keep my ears open," Rico said. "'Case I heard anything else might be fallout from that drive-by. If this shit don't look like fallout, I don't know what does."

At the corner lot, Burke saw the stone wall that bordered

the property, the dark smear down the side. He moved into the trees, Rico staying on the sidewalk. Near the wall, the ground had been kicked up, indentations in dried mud. The dark patch on the wall was blood.

"Someone came this way," he said. "They were hurting, too, bleeding. Take a look."

"Fuck that noise. These are Bruno Maglis. You want to play detective, do it your own self."

Burke squatted, looked at the blood, then the dried tracks. Two sets, one smaller than the other. Both led toward a chain-link fence. On the other side was a low white building, crime scene tape stretched along its front.

"That the place?" Burke said.

"City garage. No one uses it anymore. Unis got here, saw the lock on the gate broken, went in to check it out. Found the body."

Burke walked to the fence. Halfway up, a patch of chain-link was rust red. More blood. Someone running on adrenaline, Burke thought, to climb a fence like that with a bullet in them.

"Way it looks," Rico said, "some shit went down in that house. Mutual disagreement. Caps get popped, both men get hit. Last man standing torches the place, makes a run for it, ends up in there." He nodded at the garage.

"Maybe," Burke said. Thinking, two people came through that yard, and only one dead in the garage. That meant another man in the wind. Or a woman.

He walked back toward Rico. "Any ID with this one?"

"No."

"They do fingerprints?"

"They did."

"And?"

Rico didn't respond.

"What?" Burke said. "That three hundred I gave you wasn't enough to put us on good terms?"

"This shit gets expensive. And word is you're back working for Marquis on this one. Word is he's paying good, too."

"Word is bullshit. This guy got a sheet?"

"That," Rico said, "is the part you're gonna like." He patted his coat pocket.

Burke smiled. "Slick Rick, as always."

"Now you glad I called you?"

"I'll go a C-note more for the sheet. Another hundred when you get me what you can on the one in the house."

"That could work. For now. But you got something bigger going on, maybe you should consider cutting your old partner in."

"Nothing to cut right now. Let's see what you got."

Rico took a sheaf of folded paper from his pocket, held it out. Burke took it, opened it. The top page was a color printout of a booking photo. A hard-looking man in his forties, hair swept back, head cocked, eyefucking the photographer. Lawrence Vernon Black, with four pages of history, an arrest record going back to 1977. Armed robbery. Fraud. Assault with intent. He'd done a three-year bid in the Missouri State Penitentiary from '89 to '91 on a hijacking charge. But no arrests in the last four years, and no convictions in ten. He'd retired, or learned how not to get caught.

"What's a white boy like that doing all the way out here?" Rico said.

"Good question." Burke looked through the pages. Vital statistics, aliases, previous addresses. The most recent one was in Winter Park, Florida.

"He wasn't local," Rico said. "I'm betting the one in the house wasn't, either."

"I'd bet you're right. Name on the rental?"

"Louis Brown. At least that's what his license said."

"Good one. Lawrence Black. Louis Brown." Knowing then he'd been right all along, out-of-state pros, here to hit it and git.

"All kinds of coincidences today," Rico said.

"Haney know all this?"

"No, and if he did, he wouldn't care. Homicide's working the bodies. He wouldn't want anything to do with that mess."

"Can't blame him." Burke looked at the photo, thinking, Tough break, Mr. Lawrence Vernon Black. A heavyweight like you, ending up shot dead in the middle of nowhere. Came all the way to Detroit and never even got a chance to spend that money you stole.

"You want to take a look in that garage?" Rico said.

"No. Got what I need right here."

"I do you right?"

"You did. Anyone else know you printed these out?"

"Nah. It's just between you and me, brother."

"Let's keep it that way." Burke folded the papers, slipped them in his coat pocket.

Freeman had said it was a four-man crew, and now two of them were dead. Crossed the wrong partner, or fell out over the split. Any number of ways it could have gone bad. So at least two were left, one of them a woman. And if one of them was from Florida, another might be, too.

He flicked the cigarette at the blood on the stone wall. It sparked and died.

"Now you're contaminating a crime scene," Rico said.

"This whole city is a crime scene."

"Why we love it," Rico said.

Heading home on Eight Mile, he noticed the dark SUV about five car lengths back. It had been with him the last six miles, stayed in the same lane while other vehicles passed.

There was a plaza up ahead on the right, with a pawnshop and liquor store. Burke slowed, put on his turn signal. The SUV moved into the left lane, sped up. It was a black Dodge Durango, Michigan plates, two brothers up front, both in sunglasses and dreads. The passenger turned to look at him as they drove past.

Burke pulled into the lot, waited with the engine running, let the Durango get far ahead. If they were following him, they'd have to double back, make two U-turns to come up behind him again. There was no way to do that without giving themselves away.

His cell phone began to buzz. He got it out, didn't recognize the number. "Yeah?"

"You know who this is?" Willie Freeman's voice.

"I think so. How's the shoulder?"

"How much money we talking about?"

"For what?"

"For a name."

"You calling from the hospital?"

"No. How much money?"

"Depends. A name's just a name. If I get somewhere with it, that's different."

"I want ten grand."

"What?"

"Ten thousand for the name I give you."

"You better go easy on that Demerol, Willie. No name you can give me is worth ten grand. I probably know it already anyway."

"Maybe. Maybe not. After you left, I made some calls, found out some shit."

"Like what?"

"Ten grand, and I give the name to you, and nobody else."

"Ten's high."

"It's what I need."

"What got you so motivated all of the sudden? Damien come back to see you?"

No answer.

"He's keeping an eye on you, though, right? See if you run?"

"You want that name?"

"How do I know, five minutes after I hand over the cash, you're not on the phone to Damien?"

"Fuck him."

"Sounds like you're scared, Willie. But that's a smart way

to be right now. You did the right thing, calling me. This could work out for both of us."

"Ten grand for the name, then we done."

"Five up front. Another five if it pans out. Best I can do."

Breathing on the line. "When can you get the five?"

"Couple hours. Give it to you tonight, if you want."

"You know Brush Park? The old Presbyterian church on Woodward?"

"I know it."

"Midnight tonight. You be there with the five."

"No way. I pick the place."

"This ain't no discussion. You want the name, you be there."

Payback, Burke thought, for what he'd done at the hospital, Freeman wanting to take him over the hurdles.

"I'll think about it," he said.

"No thinking. Yes or no. Yesterday you were telling me what the deal was. Today I'm telling you."

"Midnight's too late."

"You be there twelve sharp. Five past and I'm gone."

After a moment, Burke said, "Okay. Midnight. I'll be there."

"With the cash."

"Of course. Willie, wait a minute. Don't hang up."

"What?"

"I need you to know something. What happened at the hospital. That was just business. It wasn't personal."

"Man, you got nerve to say that to me."

"But if you try to fuck with me tonight? Or don't show up? That'll be personal. And you won't need to worry about Marquis anymore, or Damien. I'll punch your clock myself, drop you in the river with a tow chain around your ankles. You feel me?"

"Just be there," Freeman said, and ended the call.

At eleven thirty, Burke pulled up outside the church. It loomed over the block like a medieval castle, high turrets and stained-glass windows. Granite steps led up to a red door. No lights inside, and no other cars on the block. He'd kept an eye on the rearview on the drive out, but there'd been no sign of the Durango.

He got out, went up the steps, saw the door was ajar. He pushed it open with a gloved hand, looked into the darkness of a vestibule.

"Walk straight ahead," a female voice said. "No need to look at me."

He turned to his left. A black woman came out of the shadows. She was heavy, wore jeans and a puffy coat. Her hair was long on one side, shaved close on the other. A dark automatic was pointed at his chest.

"I said straight ahead."

"All right." He raised his hands. "Take it easy with that thing."

"You early."

"So are you."

"Walk."

He went through the vestibule into the church, felt the woman fall in behind him. Streetlight came through the big front windows, faintly illuminated row after row of empty pews. They were laid out in a semicircle, fanning back from where the altar had once been, only a bare stretch of floor there now. The center aisle was carpeted with pigeon droppings and plaster dust. The domed ceiling was lost in shadow.

As he started down the aisle, a light flashed from an alcove. The beam moved up the aisle, climbed Burke's legs and settled on his face.

"There's good," Freeman said.

Burke stopped, raised a hand to shade his eyes. "You need to turn that thing off, Willie. Or shine it somewhere else."

The light stayed on him for another moment, then fell away, settled on the floor at his feet. Beyond the light, Freeman was only a silhouette in the darkness.

"He's alone," the woman said behind him. Burke lowered his hands.

"You got my money?" Freeman said.

"Not the way this works. You need to show yourself, Willie. I don't talk to shadows."

Freeman moved out of the alcove, into the space where the altar had been. The flashlight beam moved up again, centered on Burke's chest.

"Search him," Freeman said. "See if he got that money."

"No chance," Burke said. "In three seconds I'm going to turn around and walk out of here. Shoot me if you want. You can deal with Marquis on your own."

"You ain't doing nothing 'less I tell you to," the woman said. She came around in front of him, the gun pointed at his chest.

Burke looked past her. "That the way you're going to play this, Willie?"

"Neesa," Freeman said. "Chill."

"I don't trust this motherfucker," she said.

"Let's not make this more complicated than it is," Burke said. He reached into his right coat pocket, drew out the thick white envelope. "Your money."

The flashlight beam played across it.

"Bring it here," Freeman said.

"You want it, come get it."

Neesa came forward, the gun still on him, took the envelope, and backed away. Freeman came slow up the aisle, his breathing labored.

He wore a green field jacket draped over his shoulders, his right arm in a sling. His forehead glistened with sweat.

"You don't look so good," Burke said. "You walk out of the hospital like that?"

Freeman took the envelope from Neesa, gave her the flashlight. She shone the light on him while he opened the envelope, looked through the bills. The gun was steady in her other hand.

"You better spend some of that money on a doctor," Burke said. "You might have an infection there."

"Shut up," Neesa said.

"You need to remind your girlfriend that's only half the money," Burke said. "She shoots me, you don't get the rest."

"Neesa," Freeman said. She lowered the gun. Freeman closed the envelope, put it inside his sling.

"The name," Burke said.

Freeman leaned back against a pew. Burke could see his chest rise and fall.

"That list Marquis give you," Freeman said. "Boy named Cordell King on it?"

"He's one of them, yeah. Why?"

"Day of that stickup, he booked. No one seen him since."

"He ran?"

"That's what I said."

"Doesn't mean anything. He's probably running for the same reason you are."

Freeman shook his head. "He's new. Only been working for Marquis a few months. College boy. Always fronting tough, but he ain't shit."

"That's not worth five thousand."

"I ain't finished. Those other boys, ones that were in the Armada with me, they hiding, but they ain't far. Couple calls turned them up. Not Cordell, though. He gone."

"Marquis know that?"

"Not from me. Sooner or later, though, he will."

"Willie, you're jerking me off here."

"There's more."

"There better be."

"Back when he started with Marquis, Cordell told some boys he had a cousin was a heavy hitter. A stickup boy."

"He say his name?"

"Nah. But said his cousin worked all over. Banks, armored cars. Big scores. Said he was going to bring Cordell in on some."

"Sounds like more fronting to me."

"Few weeks back, though, he shut up about it. One of the boys that roll with me asked him about his OG cousin. Fucking with him, you know? Cordell wouldn't say shit this time."

"You think the cousin's crew shot you up, took that money?"

"Maybe."

"And you think Cordell was with them?"

"Could be."

"But you didn't see him?"

"Like I said, they had masks." He shifted, winced, rested his hip on the pew.

"You look like you're about done," Burke said.

"Don't worry about me. I told you I'd give you a name. That's the name. You check it out, see. You get me that other five thousand. Maybe I have something else for you then, too."

"Fair enough. But if all this turns out to be bullshit, I'll come back looking for my money. You know that, right?"

"I know it."

"You know where this Cordell lives?"

Freeman shook his head, looked at Neesa.

"You need to start walking," she said to Burke. "We done."

He looked at her, then at Freeman, said, "I'll be in touch," and started back up the aisle. He stopped halfway, turned. "One other thing."

"What?" Freeman said.

Burke reached under his coat, back to where the Browning .380 was tucked into his belt. He drew it out in a fluid motion, the gun coming up smoothly, not snagging on anything. Neesa saw it, started to raise her gun, and he shot her twice in the chest.

The shots sounded almost as one, echoed through the church. Pigeons burst from the balcony, flew off, and disappeared into darkness. The flashlight hit the floor, rolled against a pew. Burke pointed the Browning at Freeman. "Stay right there, sport."

Neesa lay on her back, not moving. Burke kicked her gun away, then bent and picked up the flashlight, turned its beam on Freeman. He was frozen.

"You think you're smarter than me, Willie." He settled the beam on Freeman's chest. "But you're not." He aimed the Browning at the circle of light, squeezed the trigger.

The shot knocked Freeman off the pew. Burke tracked him with the flashlight as he fell, fired twice more, the echoes chasing themselves. Brass clinked on marble.

Behind Burke, the woman groaned. He shone the light on her. She was blinking, her eyes unfocused, blood on her lips. He knelt, fit the muzzle of the Browning up under her jaw and fired once.

He used the flashlight to find all the casings, dropped them into a pocket. Then he turned Freeman's body over, took the envelope from his sling, careful to avoid the blood.

He put the envelope away, turned off the flashlight and tossed it into the shadows, heard it break. Then he walked up the aisle in the pale light from the stained glass, through the vestibule, and back out into the night.

FIFTEEN

Driving back from the mall, Crissa let the little girl have her silence. She was looking out the window, the breeze in her hair. In her lap was the new iPod Crissa had bought her, still in its packaging. It was a children's model, with a Mickey Mouse design on the case. At the electronics store, Crissa had asked the clerk to load it with songs a six-year-old might like. When he asked her for suggestions, she had none.

Haley hadn't talked much on the ride there, had never asked where they were going. When Crissa bought pizza slices and orange drinks at the food court, Haley had eaten in silence but left nothing on her plate. When they were done, Crissa took her to a children's store, let her pick out two new sets of clothes, including a Mickey Mouse T-shirt to match the iPod, Crissa guessing her size. Realizing she had no idea what a six-year-old might wear, what she might listen to or watch on TV.

She'd let Crissa take her hand as they were leaving the store. Toys "R" Us was next, and they'd left with a new Barbie doll, a stuffed squirrel, and a pink vinyl backpack. She had to be coaxed to pick out things. The doll had been Crissa's idea, remembering the broken one on the floor of the empty house. Haley had thanked her as they'd left the mall but had never smiled.

Now, in the car, the bags at her feet, Haley was tapping one foot on the floorboard, swinging the other. Humming to herself.

"Hey," Crissa said. When she didn't answer, Crissa touched her on the shoulder. Haley looked at her.

"How you doin' there?" Crissa said.

"Thank you for all the presents."

"You said that already. You're welcome." Crissa reached out, brushed hair from her eyes. "Next time, maybe we can go somewhere, do something about this mop."

"What's that on your arm?"

"What?"

Haley pointed at her left wrist, the Chinese character there. "That."

Crissa looked at the tattoo, the faint burn scar that ran across it.

"That's there to remind me of someone who was very close to me. He has one, too, just like it."

"What's it say?"

"It's the Chinese word for 'perseverance.' Do you know what that means?"

Haley shook her head.

"It means to keep going when there's something you want, or something you need. Not giving up, even when things get rough and it feels like you can't go on anymore."

"It's pretty." She looked out the window again.

"So you like Mickey and Minnie, huh?" Crissa said. "They your favorites?"

"And Donald and Goofy. Pluto, too."

"Have you ever been to Disney World?"

"No. Mom says it's too far away."

"It's not that far. Closer than you think. Maybe we'll go there someday."

"Who?"

"Me and you. How's that sound?" Regretting it as soon as she said it.

Haley nodded again but didn't smile, looked back out the window. She doesn't believe me, Crissa thought. And why should she?

The sky was a hard blue, the clouds gone. They passed a horse farm, the horses loose in a big pasture. Haley craned her head to see them, put her hand out the window and waved.

What are you doing here? Crissa thought. This isn't your daughter, your family. You need to do what you came to do and move on.

She felt a touch on her arm, turned. Haley was looking at her. "Are you sad?"

"What?"

"You're crying."

"No," Crissa said. "It's just the sun down here. I'm not used to it."

Haley pointed at the sunglasses hanging from the rear-view.

"Right," Crissa said. "That's a good idea, isn't it?" She took them down, wiped her eyes with her wrist.

"It's okay to be sad," Haley said.

"Is that right?"

"Sometimes."

"Are you sad?"

"Not now."

"That's good," Crissa said, and turned away, not wanting her to see the tears. She put on the sunglasses.

When they pulled into the motel lot, Haley grew quiet. Crissa saw where she was looking. There were two motorcycles parked at the edge of the lot, near the far stairs. Flat-black Harleys with chrome pipes.

She parked, turned the engine off. The door to 216 was ajar. "Haley, wait here, all right?"

Crissa got out of the car. She started for the far stairs, heard the car door open and close behind her, turned to see Haley following.

"Go back to the car," Crissa said. Haley shook her head, caught up with her, took her hand.

"All right," Crissa said. "But stay close to me." She hoisted her up, surprised by her weight, carried her up the stairwell to the second floor.

When she set her down, she let Haley take her left hand, wanting to keep the right free. She knocked on the door, and it opened wider, Claudette standing there. She gave Crissa a look she couldn't read, then stepped aside.

There were two men on the couch, both with long hair, sleeveless denim jackets over leather, engineer boots. Roy stood against the wall on the other side of the room, arms folded, chewing his lip. He looked up as Crissa came in.

The man on the right, grayer than the other, with a full beard, said, "Hey, baby." Crissa looked at him, felt Haley move behind her. Realized then who he meant.

"Come sit on daddy's lap," he said, and patted his knee.

Haley tightened her grip on Crissa's hand. She squeezed back.

"Company," the other one said. He was younger, had a broken nose and long sideburns. He looked at Roy. "You should have told us."

"Which one of you is Blue?" Crissa said.

The younger one looked at her, said, "I don't believe we've met."

"Claudette," Crissa said, "why don't you take Haley down to that Dairy Queen up the block, get some ice cream?"

"Why you wanna do that?" the older one said. "She just got here." He smiled at Haley, showed a gold tooth. "Come on over here, beautiful. Give Uncle Jackson a kiss."

Haley squeezed her hand tighter. Crissa looked at Claudette, said, "Take her."

"Now, that's no way to be," Jackson said. "Look, you're getting her all upset."

Claudette came behind Crissa, took Haley's free hand, tried to lead her away.

"Come on, sweetie," Jackson said. "Sit over here."

Crissa knelt, gently worked her fingers free from Haley's. "Go with your mom. I'll see you in a few minutes." Haley shook her head.

"Let's go," Claudette said. "Ice cream." When Haley didn't move, Crissa scooped her up, carried her out the door, Claudette following. She set her down, kissed the top of her head. "Stay with your mom. Go on, go get some ice cream. I'll be over in a little bit."

"I don't have any money," Claudette said. Crissa took a twenty from her pocket, handed it to her. "Stay there. I'll come find you when they're gone."

"What are you going to do?"

"Just go."

Haley was wiping her eyes. Crissa squeezed her shoulder, felt the bones there, so close beneath the skin.

"Go on now. Everything's okay. I'll come get you in a little while."

She watched them walk away, hand in hand. Haley turned to look back over her shoulder at Crissa. Claudette picked her up, carried her down the stairs and out of sight.

Crissa went back into the room, closed the door. The two bikers were watching her. Roy was still by the wall, swaying back and forth, arms crossed, hands in his armpits.

To Blue, she said, "How much does he owe you?"

"Like I said, lady. I don't think we've met."

"Hey, Roy," Jackson said. "How come this chick knows your shit?"

"Shut up," Blue said. Then to her, "What makes you think he owes me anything?"

"We can dick around here or get down to it," she said. "How much to get free and clear?"

"Free and clear," Blue said, and sat back. "That sounds nice. Free and clear. Who wouldn't want to be that?"

Jackson got up, started for the door. She moved in front of him. He frowned. "What are you doing?"

She could smell the alcohol on him. Aim for the throat or eyes, she thought. Anywhere else and he might not feel it. And you'll only get one shot before they're both all over you.

"Hey, Jackie," the other one said. "Sit down. Be cool."

Jackson squinted at her. She didn't look away, watched for the shoulder movement that meant he was about to swing on her, hoped it would give her enough time to hit him first.

He turned away from her, sat back on the couch.

Blue looked at Roy. "What's going on here, *papi*?"

Roy shrugged. "She's a friend of Haley's father."

Jackson said, "Dude, I thought *you* were her father."

"Her real father," Roy said.

"Enough of this," she said. "How much?"

Blue pulled an earlobe, looked at her. She saw the tattoos just below the knuckles of his right hand, PAIN spelled out in Gothic letters.

"How much," she said, "for you to leave them alone?"

"These are friends of mine you're talking about," Blue said. "Claudette and I go back a long way. I know her when she used to dance at the Whisky Room. She was fine back then, let me tell you. But if you're talking business . . ."

"I didn't tell her anything," Roy said. "I don't know where—"

"Shut up," Blue said. Then to her, "I'm not saying I know what you're talking about here. But if he has debts, why wouldn't he take care of them himself?"

"You're a smart guy," she said. "A businessman. But he's a fuckup." She nodded at Roy. He was chewing his lip again, watching her.

"You know you'll never get more than chump change out of him," she said. "Even if he squares up this time, it'll happen again. He's a junkie. It's their nature."

Blue laughed, looked at Roy. "She's sure got your number, slick." Jackson still looked confused.

"She's got money," Roy said, talking fast, the words spilling out. "A lot. She brought it here for us. From Haley's father." She looked at him. He took a step back.

"Is that right? Now I'm interested," Blue said. "And you're right, *chica*, he's a fuckup, but so what?"

"I know he's been dealing for you. I know he owes you money. He can't pay it now, and probably won't be able to anytime soon. Squeeze him as much as you want, it won't make any difference."

"That's his business, isn't it?"

"Yours, too, if you want to get paid. Here's the offer. I pay you what he owes, plus a little extra for your troubles. You cut your losses, walk away."

"Where's the money?" Jackson said. "Let's see it." She ignored him.

"Keep talking," Blue said.

"There's nothing else to say. It's a one time only offer. Tomorrow I'm gone."

"Man, what is all this shit?" Jackson said. "This is crazy talk."

"Maybe not so crazy," Blue said. Then to her, "You know how much he owes?"

"In the ballpark."

"Ballpark, huh? Maybe it's a bigger ballpark than you think."

She shook her head. "You wouldn't trust him with serious money. You're no fool. You've dealt with people like him before."

"Yeah, I have." He nodded at Roy. "How'd this guy get so lucky, get a fine lady like you looking after him, paying his debts?"

"It's not about him."

"The woman, then. Or no, the little girl, right? You family or something?"

"No."

"What, then? You're just doing a good deed?"

"I'm making you a deal. Question is, are you smart enough to take it?"

Jackson leaned forward. "This bitch needs to get slapped, Blue. Why we listening to this?"

Blue looked at Roy, then back at her, said, "Ten thousand."

"No way it's that much," she said. "Not for O-Bombs. I heard two, three at the most."

"Yeah, where'd you hear that?"

"Fuck this," Jackson said. He got up and went into the kitchenette. They heard him opening and closing cabinets.

"Five," she said. "And we're all of us squared. How's that?"

"Five?" Blue said. "What about my time and trouble? You think I like having to come out to this shithole every week, track down our friend here to get my money? You don't think my time's valuable?"

"Six, then. For your trouble. That's probably twice what he owes you, enough to cover any vig."

"Then let me guess, we don't take your deal, you go to the law, right? That what you gonna say next?"

"No."

"Or maybe we take the deal, and you go to the law anyway."

"I wouldn't do that. A deal is a deal."

Jackson came out of the kitchen, shaking a box of graham crackers.

"Shit's stale, bro," he said to Roy. "This the same box as last time?"

He leaned in the doorway, took out a cracker, bit off a piece, made a face, and dropped it back in the box.

"How do I know what you'd do or wouldn't do?" Blue said. "You say you're gonna give me six grand in cash. I could be setting myself up. You might be the G yourself, all I know."

"I might be."

"So make it seven."

"Make it six."

"You got a way about you, I'll say that. What are the chances we get to know each other a little better?"

"I don't trust this broad," Jackson said. He dropped the box on the floor. "I don't trust her at all."

"No, she's okay," Blue said. "She just thinks she has to act tough to get by, right?" He looked at Crissa. "But maybe under all that, not so tough after all."

"What's your answer?"

"Six it is. When can you get it?"

"Tonight. Like I said, after tomorrow I'm gone."

"You're not gonna stick around, see if we hold up our part of the deal, lay off your friend here?"

"He's no friend of mine," she said. "But yes, I trust you. I'll have to, won't I?" Lying.

"Then I guess we got a deal," Blue said. He stood.

"Ten o'clock tonight," she said. "Here."

"I don't need to tell you, if there's cops around, or I see any shit at all I don't like, it'll be bad fucking news for these people. The little girl, too. Even if it's some vice cop busting a tranny hooker downstairs. I see law around, I walk, and you deal with the consequences."

"Understood. One thing." She tilted her head at Jackson. "Don't bring him."

"Jacky? He's harmless. He just likes them a little young, is all. He'll find himself another girlfriend soon."

She felt a flush of heat in her face, a tightness in her gut.

Blue looked at Roy, said, "Look like *chica* here saved your ass."

Roy didn't respond. Blue looked at Jackson, said, "Come on, hoss. We got other stops to make."

She moved away from the door. Jackson eyed her as he went past

"Tonight," Blue said. "I'm looking forward to it." They went out.

After a moment, she followed them onto the balcony, watched as they went down to the motorcycles, climbed on and kickstarted the engines. Their exhaust blew leaves and grit off the blacktop.

They wheeled the bikes around, headed for the exit. Neither wore a helmet. As they waited for a break in the traffic, Jackson looked back. He made a pistol with his right hand, pointed it up at her.

Blue pulled out onto the street, sped away, Jackson following. She listened to the roar of their engines as it faded.

Roy came out behind her.

She turned to him and said, "Pack."

She took them to another motel a mile away, got them checked into a second-floor room, paid cash in advance. Everything they had was in two suitcases and a black garbage bag with a red twist-tie.

Haley sat on one of the beds. She'd taken the Barbie out of its box, was combing its hair with a pink plastic comb. Claudette sat beside her. Roy paced.

Crissa nodded at the suitcases. "That's it, huh?"

Claudette rubbed a bare arm. "We had to leave a lot behind when we left the house. Traveling light, I guess."

"She didn't have any more dolls? Toys?"

"Things get lost along the way. You know the way kids are."

Roy said, "We need to talk about all this. Now."

"Right," Crissa said. "Let's take a ride. We'll pick up some food, bring it back."

"That's not what I meant."

"I know what you meant. We'll talk in the car."

To Claudette, she said, "Don't leave the room. If something comes up, call me on the cell. We won't be long."

Haley didn't look up. She was combing the doll's hair with careful concentration, as if no one else were there.

On the stairs, Crissa let Roy get ahead of her. When they reached the bottom, she said, "Hey."

He turned. He was standing in front of an alcove with vending machines and an icemaker.

"Yeah?" he said, and she straight-armed him in the chest, drove him back against the soda machine, rocked it.

"What the fuck?" he said.

"I ought to let them kill you."

He came forward, and she shoved him back again. She set herself, wondering if he'd come at her. Instead, he took another step back, rubbed his shoulder. Behind him, the ice machine clattered and hummed.

"Answer me now and answer me straight," she said. "Did either of those two ever touch Haley?"

"No."

"Look at me. You never handed her over, some week you were short on what you owed?"

"I'd never do that."

She moved toward him, fighting the instinct to close the distance quick, hit him as hard as she could. He retreated until his back was against the ice machine.

"You ever leave them alone with her?" she said.

"No, I swear."

"But you thought about it, right? Using her to get you out of trouble, save you from a beating? Because she's not your daughter anyway, right?"

"I screwed up, I know. But I wouldn't do that."

"I hope you're telling the truth. Because if I find out you're not—"

"Ask Claudette. You think she'd let me do something like that?"

"You two, I don't know what to think."

When she turned away, he said, "What are we going to do?"

She looked back at him. "About what?"

"About the money. About tonight."

"I'll worry about that," she said. "Get in the car."

SIXTEEN

At nine o'clock, she was parked at the Sunoco station, head lights and engine off. The lights in 216 were on, the curtain drawn. A chill in the air, and no one out in the parking lot. She could hear muffled music behind one of the second-floor doors, knew it had to be loud inside. That was good.

She clenched and unclenched her fingers inside the gloves, the adrenaline working in her already. There was a sourness in her stomach, the acid taste of bile in her throat.

At nine thirty, a beat-up Dodge with a dented passenger door rolled into the lot, Jackson driving, Blue beside him. They'd left the motorcycles behind. Too recognizable, too noisy, for what they'd come to do.

They circled the lot slowly, then drove back into the service alley, parked beside the Dumpster, killed the lights and engine.

They'll sit there for a while, she thought, keep an eye out in case it's a setup, see if there's anyone around who doesn't belong. She saw the flare of a match inside the car, the glow of a cigarette.

She took a deep breath, held it, tightening her hips and stomach, gripped the wheel to steady her hands.

Just before ten, they got out of the car, stood there talking. A cat raced out from behind the Dumpster, crossed their path, and disappeared into high weeds.

When they moved into the light at the base of the stairwell, she saw Blue had a short-barreled revolver in his hand. He opened the cylinder to check the loads, closed it again, said something to Jackson. They started up the stairs.

She let out her breath. You should drive away, she thought. Go back to the hotel, get the rest of the money and your things, buy a train ticket, head north, head home. The smart thing. What Wayne would do. No percentage in staying here. But then there was the girl . . .

They came out of the stairwell onto the second-floor walkway, taking their time, being quiet about it. She'd wedged a folded matchbook into the strike plate of 216, so the door would open with a push. She wanted them inside the room. It would give her more time.

On the seat beside her was a manila envelope thick with cash—six thousand dollars in banded bills. She'd sealed it with rubber bands. The envelope went into the inside pocket of her dark zippered jacket. Then she reached behind for the aluminum baseball bat on the floor. She'd bought the bat and jacket at a sporting goods store on the way here.

She'd turned off the courtesy light, so the car stayed dark as she got out. She let the door close without latching, started across the lot.

There was a shadowed area between the motel wall and the Dumpster, and she waited there, picturing Blue and Jackson up in the room, angry, going through closets and dressers, realizing they were gone for good.

She heard the door open again, boot heels on the walkway above her. Fast, not caring about noise now. They came down the stairwell, Jackson in front. She saw the dull glint of the gun in his left hand, another revolver.

When he reached the bottom step, she moved away from the wall. Jackson said, "Hey, Blue, here she is—" and then he saw the bat.

He got his left hand up as she swung. The bat cracked into his elbow, sent the revolver flying across the blacktop. He doubled with pain, and then Blue was coming down behind him, pushing him out of the way, gun up.

She swung, aimed for the outside of his left knee, felt the impact all the way to her shoulders. The leg flew out from under him, and he went down hard. She swung at the gun, missed, and got his wrist on the backswing. The gun hit the wall, landed at her feet. She kicked it toward the Dumpster, turned to meet Jackson coming at her.

She feinted at his head. When he raised his right arm to block it, she checked her movement, dropped her shoulder and swung hard into his ribs on the left side, felt them crack. He bent, and she sidestepped and swung low, laid the bat across his shins. He cried out, went down.

Blue was on his knees now, crabbing toward the stairs to pull himself up. She brought the bat down on his right shoulder like an ax. He grunted, tried to roll away and cover up. Behind her, Jackson was moaning, "You bitch. You fucking bitch."

She went back to stand over him. She was breathing hard. "You touch that little girl?" she said.

"What?"

"I said, did you touch her?"

"Fuck you."

"Wrong answer," she said, and swung the bat across his left knee. He screamed, gripped his leg, rolled onto his side, rocking slowly back and forth.

Blue had worked himself into a sitting position, his back against the stairs. His right arm hung useless. He grinned, his teeth outlined in blood. He'd cut something inside his mouth when he'd fallen.

She turned to him, had to catch her breath before she could speak. "I'd tell you to stay away from those people, but it wouldn't make any difference, would it?"

He shook his head, spit blood at her. She stepped back to avoid it.

"Didn't think so," she said, and swung the bat into his left ankle. He rolled, tried to cover his head, and she used the bat on his body twice more, then backed away, dizzy and reeling.

She looked back at Jackson. He was still on the ground, whimpering, tears on his face. She tossed the bat away. It clanged and rolled on the blacktop. She pulled the envelope of cash from her pocket, dropped it near Blue's head.

"My part of the deal," she said. "You're paid off. No need to come around here anymore."

She found the revolvers, unloaded them, dropped the shells into a storm drain. The guns went into another drain twenty feet away. Still breathing hard, she walked back to the gas station, Jackson crying softly on the ground behind her.

Back in the car, she tried to steady her breathing. Then she felt the hot rush coming up, got the door open just in time, and vomited onto the blacktop.

When Claudette opened the door, Crissa said, "Get your things together. We're leaving."

Haley was asleep on one of the beds, fully dressed, stuffed squirrel held tight. Roy sprang up from where he'd been sitting in a corner chair, said, "What happened?"

She ignored him, said to Claudette, "Call your sister. Make sure she's home. We're going there tonight."

"Why?"

"Not a good idea to stay around town right now. Better we get moving."

"What did you do?" Roy said.

She looked at him. "What you should have."

"Oh, shit," he said, "oh, shit," and sat back down again.

Claudette hadn't moved. "Did you kill them?"

"No," Crissa said. "But they won't be back on their bikes for a while. Don't fight me on this. We need to get going."

Roy had his head in his hands, looking at the floor. "I could have taken care of it. I could have." He looked up at her. "You really did it this time, didn't you?"

Crissa looked at Claudette, said, "Make that call."

"It was all settled," he said. "We had a deal."

"They didn't come to deal," she said. "They came to kill all of us, take whatever money they could find."

"You don't know that."

To Claudette, she said, "Up to you whether he comes or not."

Claudette looked at Roy.

"Wait a goddamn minute," he said. "What do you mean, it's up to her?"

"You can stay in town, all I care," Crissa said to him. "But I wouldn't advise it."

"Don't listen to her," he said to Claudette. "We're not going anywhere."

"I settled your debt," Crissa said. "You want to stay around here, be my guest. But in a day or two, they—or more likely some friends of theirs—are going to come around looking for payback. And they'll be looking for you."

"Payback? Why?"

"You want to take him along," she said to Claudette, "we'll take him. But my advice is don't."

"And what the fuck am I supposed to do?" he said.

Haley stirred, opened her eyes. Claudette sat beside her, stroked her hair, didn't look at Roy.

Crissa took an envelope from her jacket pocket. "There's a thousand in there." She tossed it on the other bed. "Enough to get you away from here. Plane, train, bus, whatever. If you're smart, you'll leave Florida."

"A thousand? I deserve a lot more than that."

"You're lucky you got anything. Take it and be glad."

"Claudette, don't let her do this."

She looked at him now. "I'm sorry, Roy. But she's right. I've been thinking about it since all this started. We need to do what's best for Haley. She needs to be safe."

"She *is* safe. She's always been safe with me. What are you talking about? I'd never do anything to hurt her."

Haley sat up. Claudette put an arm around her. "I'm sorry, Roy. I am. But maybe being apart is best right now. For a while at least."

He stood. "She put this in your head, didn't she? Turned you against me."

"It's more than that, Roy. It has been for a while."

Crissa watched him, ready to get between them if needed.

"I can't believe this," he said. "Why are you doing this to me?"

"The room's paid for the night," Crissa told him. "You can stay if you want. But tomorrow morning, first thing, you need to get moving."

"This isn't right. We're a family. We should be together."

"A little late for that," Crissa said.

"This is fucked."

"Maybe down the road, it'll be different," Claudette said. "But right now, Roy, we both have some things we need to take care of. On our own. You know that, too. Then maybe later . . ."

Crissa let that sit, said to Roy, "Take the money or not. It's up to you."

Haley was curled against her mother now, still holding the squirrel.

"You should get a coat for her," Crissa said. "It's getting cool out."

Roy picked up the envelope, opened it, looked at the bills inside. "So this is it," he said. "After everything I've done."

"I'm sorry, Roy," Claudette said.

He closed the envelope, looked at Crissa. "This isn't over."

"You better hope it is," she said. "For your sake." Then to Claudette, "Make that call. I want to get on the road. We've got a long way to go."

SEVENTEEN

Cordell King's apartment was in a redbrick building on the West Side. Five stories, a vacant weedy lot on one side, an empty, fenced-in playground on the other. Burke cruised past, saw a few parked cars, but no one on the street. Everyone at work or in school.

He drove to the end of the block, turned down a side street, and parked. It had cost Burke another fifty, but Rico had run the name that morning, come up with the address. There wasn't much on his sheet; arrests for possession of stolen property, a misdemeanor marijuana offense. If he'd been on the crew that hit Marquis he was batting out of his league. The sheet said he was twenty-four, but in the booking photo he looked fifteen.

Burke killed the engine, lit a Newport. A back alley, just big enough for a garbage truck, ran the length of the block.

No cars were parked here, and the ones out front had been empty. If Marquis had the address and had people watching it, they were keeping their heads down. Or they'd already been here and gone.

He got out of the car, locked the doors, and started up the alley. The Browning was a weight in his overcoat pocket.

Overflowing trash cans back here. Broken glass and crack vials on the ground. The rear door to Cordell's building was metal with reinforced glass. Burke flicked his cigarette away, got out the slim wallet of lockpick tools, used the pick and pressure wrench. He worked the lock gently, careful not to break off the pick, and the tumblers gave way with a click.

He put the wallet away, eased the door open, waited. No alarm. He went through into a hallway, pulled the door shut behind him.

To the left, a stairwell. To the right, an elevator and a door marked MANAGER, TV noise inside. The hallway ran straight to the front door. He could see the empty street beyond.

He went up the stairs slowly, distributing his weight so they didn't creak. He took thin leather gloves from his coat pocket, pulled them on. At the fourth floor, he got out the Browning, held it at his side.

Three doors on each side, odd numbers to the left, even to the right. He stood outside 410, knocked and listened. There was no sound within. He knocked again, then stuck the gun into his belt, got out the lockpick tools again. He worked the doorknob first, then the dead bolt. Still no sound inside. He put the picks away, took out the Browning, toed the door open a few inches. No chain.

Silence. He opened the door wider. Out came the stale odor of marijuana, and something else bitter and harsh. Sweat and sickness.

He went in, shut the door behind him. In the living room was an orange futon, a spool coffee table with burn marks, an ashtray half full of marijuana roaches. On one wall, a Bob Marley poster. On another, a map of Africa in red, black, and green. Slats of daylight came through gaps in the venetian blinds. The blinds hung unevenly, one side lower than the other. Dust motes swirled in the light.

Beyond the living room was a kitchenette, then a short hallway. At the end, a half-closed door. He could hear faint breathing within, irregular and ragged.

The gun at his side, he moved down the hall. A bathroom door was open on the left. He looked in. The floor was littered with patches of bloody gauze, surgical tape. An empty hydrogen peroxide bottle lay on its side. In the tub, a white towel stained dark with blood.

At the bedroom door, he stopped, listened to the breathing within, then a low moan. He put the fingers of his left hand against the wood, waited another moment, then pushed the door open, and raised the gun.

The room was dim, a shade pulled down over the only window. Light crept in around its edges. A young black man lay in the bed, bare-chested, a single sheet pulled up past his waist. The room stank.

"Cordell . . . that you?" The voice weak. Burke pointed the gun at him, sidestepped away from the door. No one else in the room.

Burke felt for a light switch on the wall. flicked it on. The man, a kid really, closed his eyes, turned his head away. On the floor lay a vomit-stained pillow and a pair of bloody jeans. A dark hoodie, the left side stiff with blood, hung on a chair.

The kid looked back at him, blinking in the light, said, "Who are you?" Burke put the gun away, came closer. On the nightstand was a bent, burned spoon, a votive candle, a length of rubber tubing and a plastic syringe.

"You a doctor?" the kid said. His eyes were the pale yellow of old bone.

Burke lifted the sheet, and the smell rose up. The kid was naked and had a bandage on his stomach, just above his left hip, soaked through with blood. He was trembling, skin wet with sweat. There was blood on the sheet beneath him, and Burke caught a whiff of ruptured bowel. He covered him again.

"I need a doctor," the kid said.

"Yeah. You do." He opened the nightstand drawer. Inside was a blued revolver, two small bindles of aluminum foil. Another piece of foil lay on the floor, open and empty.

"You got to help me," the kid said.

There was a closet in the room. Burke opened the sliding door, pushed hanging clothes aside. No suitcases or bags, nothing but blankets on the top shelf. He tapped the walls and floor. Solid.

He turned the jeans over with his foot, saw the bulge of the wallet in the back pocket. He took it out, opened it. Inside were two twenty-dollar bills, a credit card, and a photo driver's license in the name Kevin Ferron, with a West Side address.

Burke pocketed the twenties and the license, dropped the wallet on the floor. He'd search the apartment, but knew he'd find no money here. Cordell would have it, wherever he was.

In the living room, he went to the window, parted the blinds, and looked out. Halfway down the block on the opposite side, the black Durango was parked at the curb. He could see the two men inside. He hadn't spotted them on his way here, so if they'd followed him, they were getting better at it. He wondered if they'd try to come up or just sit out there, wait for him. Follow him wherever he went next. Let him do all the work.

He went back in the bedroom. "Where's Cordell?"

"I need that doctor."

"Tell me where Cordell is, and I'll call one." He lifted the bloodstained hoodie from the chair with two fingers, dropped it on the floor, pulled the chair closer to the bed. "You're in bad shape. You know that, right?"

Ferron's eyes closed, opened. "Water."

"You're gut shot, kid. Water'll kill you."

Burke took an aluminum bindle from the drawer, opened it. Inside was a pea-sized piece of dark sludge. Black tar heroin. He showed it to the kid. "You want this?"

Ferron nodded.

"Let me guess. Cordell gave you the first shot to keep you quiet, right? Then left the rest for you. Raw deal, him running out on you like that. Left you behind, took all that money. That what happened?"

Ferron nodded again, raised a hand weakly off the bed, let it fall again.

"Long time since I've seen anybody do this, but I'll figure it out," Burke said. "Some things you don't forget, right? We'll get you straight, then we'll get a doctor up here, get you to a hospital. Just tell me where Cordell is."

"Said he was going to call . . . get an ambulance."

"Guess he forgot, huh? How long you been here?"

Ferron shook his head. He didn't know.

Burke went into the bathroom, filled a Dixie cup with water, brought it back into the bedroom. Ferron looked at it. Burke set it down on the nightstand, depressed the syringe, and put the needle in the water. He drew the plunger back, watched the syringe fill, then set it beside the candle.

"Sooner you tell me," he said, "sooner I can help you out."

Ferron shuddered. "It's cold."

"This'll warm you right up," Burke said. He dropped the heroin into the spoon, squirted in water. "But first things first, right?"

Ferron looked at the spoon. Burke leaned forward, said, "If you're not ready to talk about Cordell, tell me about the woman."

Ferron squinted, confused.

"Were you part of the crew that took down Marquis's stash? His drop car?" Burke said.

Ferron shook his head.

"But Cordell was, wasn't he?" He squirted the rest of the water from the syringe onto the floor.

"Yeah."

"And then you two, you took the money away from the others, right? The ones that stole it?"

Ferron tried to wet his lips. "I need that spike, man."

"You'll get it. One of them was a woman, right?"

"Yeah."

"How much of the money did she get?"

"Half."

"How much was that?"

"A hundred and eighty."

"That what you and Cordell got, too?"

He nodded.

"See, that's just the kind of shit I want to know." He got out his lighter, lit the votive candle, set the spoon across the rim.

"Now what you need to do," Burke said, "is tell me everything you know about the woman, everything you heard, everything Cordell said."

While Ferron talked, Burke kept one eye on the spoon. The water turned dark and began to bubble. "Almost there," he said.

"I don't know anything else," Ferron said. "I told you everything." He looked at the spoon, the vapor rising from it.

"Good enough," Burke said. He picked up the syringe. "You probably use cotton as a filter, right? But I don't think we need to bother with that this time." He dipped the tip of the needle into the spoon, drew out dark liquid until the spoon was empty. He tapped the syringe, squirted fluid to clear the needle. He set the syringe back on the night stand, took out the rubber tubing.

Ferron held out his left arm. Burke could see the tracks there, just below the elbow. He tied the tubing around the upper arm, knotted it, popped a finger on the skin there.

"You've still got good veins," Burke said. "You're young."
He sat back then, crossed his arms. "So where is he? He
couldn't have gotten far. He have family around here?"

Ferron shook his head.

"A baby mama? A girlfriend?"

"Maybe. Maybe that's where he went."

"Maybe won't cut it, Kevin. Not if you want some of this
good stuff here. Is that where he was going?"

Ferron nodded.

Burke held the syringe where Ferron could see it. "A name.
And an address."

When Ferron was done talking, Burke took his wrist, gently extended the arm. He traced the point of the needle until
it was atop a ridged vein, slid it in. He depressed the plunger
slowly, then pulled it back a little so blood flowed into the
syringe. Then he pushed the plunger all the way home, until
the syringe was empty.

"There we go, son," he said quietly. "There we go." He took
out the syringe, untied the tubing.

Ferron shuddered, closed his eyes.

Burke opened the other bindle, went through the same
process again. When he had the syringe full, he took Ferron's
wrist again. Ferron made a small noise but didn't open his
eyes. Burke gave him the second shot in the same place,
pushed the plunger home, left the needle there. Ferron shuddered again, then lay still.

Burke went to the window, moved the blinds aside, looked
down. The Durango was still there.

He locked the apartment behind him, rode the elevator

down, and went out the front door. He crossed the yard toward the Durango. The two men inside watched him as he neared. He went around to the driver's side, made a rolling motion with his left hand.

The driver powered down his window, looked out at him. It was the same man Burke had seen on Eight Mile. Sunglasses, dreads.

"How's it going?" Burke said. He could see his own reflection in the sunglass lenses. The driver looked down at him, didn't respond.

"You work for Marquis?" Burke said.

"Who?" the driver said.

Burke squinted, looked up and down the street. Still no one around.

"Biggest dope dealer in Wayne County, dozens of soldiers on the street, and he still comes to me to solve his problems," Burke said. "What's that tell you?"

The driver looked at him for a long moment, said, "You need to step off."

"If you're looking for Cordell, he's not here. And I don't think he's coming back, either. Or is it just me you're following?"

The driver looked at his partner, then back at Burke. "Get the fuck out of here, man. I ain't gonna tell you again."

"I believe you," Burke said. He drew the Browning from his coat and shot the driver in the temple. His head snapped to the side, blood spattered the inside of the windshield. The sunglasses landed on the dashboard.

The passenger clawed at his waistband. Burke leaned farther

in the window, pushed the driver aside, pointed the gun at him. He stopped reaching, raised his hands. He was younger than the driver.

"Put your hands on the dashboard," Burke said. "What's your name?"

The passenger looked at the gun, did as he was told. "New York."

"New York? That your street name?"

"Yeah."

"Okay, New York. Marquis send you to follow me?"

He nodded.

"He looking for Cordell?"

"Man, I don't know shit about Cordell. Damien just told us to keep an eye on you, see where you go."

A yellow school bus came down the street. Burke leaned casually against the Durango's door, gun below the window line. The bus passed without slowing. It was empty, no faces at the windows.

"Damien say why he put you on me?" Burke said.

"No."

"And you never asked?"

"That ain't my nevermind."

Burke nodded, looked through the blood-dotted windshield. The bus halted at a stop sign, turned left.

"So you're not after the money?" Burke said.

"What money?"

"The money that got took."

"I don't know anything about that."

Burke shook his head. "That fucking guy."

"What guy?"

"Marquis. Always putting me in an awkward position, much as I try to help him."

"Listen, I got no beef with you, man. Whatever's going on with you and Marquis, that's between you two."

"That's right." Burke raised the gun and fired twice, the noise filling the Durango. Gunsmoke drifted against the inside of the windshield, floated away.

He put the gun away, opened the door. A shell casing fell out onto the street. There was another in the driver's lap, a third on the floor near the gas pedal. He dropped them all in a coat pocket.

Another school bus coming toward him, this one empty as well. He kept his face averted, as if talking to someone inside the Durango. He waited for the bus to pass and turn at the corner. Then he walked back to his car.

EIGHTEEN

When the woman left the apartment, Burke tossed what was left of his cigarette, watched her walk the flagstone path to the parking lot. Black girl, midtwenties, straight hair cut in bangs, designer blouse and jeans. Sunlight glinted on a thick gold necklace.

Late afternoon, and he'd been parked here for an hour, watching the pale green door to apartment 105. The address Ferron had given him wasn't what he'd expected. These were garden apartments, almost all the way out to Troy. Neat lawns, flower beds. He'd come directly here, worried that Cordell might be on the move again soon. He'd parked the Impala in a visitor's spot across the lot, waited for someone to come out that door.

The woman got into a Honda Civic with a University of

Michigan decal in the rear window. She started the engine, backed out of the spot. He watched her drive past. She never looked in his direction.

He waited another five minutes, to see if anyone else came out. The complex was two identical buildings linked by an outdoor staircase and breezeway. Apartment 105 opened into the common area in the center of the complex. One window faced the parking lot, shades drawn.

No telling when the woman might be back, so he had to take his chances, move fast. He got out of the car, went up the path. There was a spyhole in the door of 105. He knocked, stepped back and to the side. If Cordell was inside, he was probably armed, might be jittery and frightened enough to lose his shit, start shooting through the door.

He knocked again, louder, right hand on the Browning in his coat pocket. He tried the doorbell then, held his thumb on it, heard the buzzing inside the apartment. A series of quick stabs, then holding it down again, letting anyone inside know he wasn't going away.

Footsteps on the other side. Burke said, "Detroit Police. Open the door."

The spyhole darkened, someone looking out.

"You need to open up," Burke said. "Or I'm going to get the manager, have him open it."

"What do you want?" A man's voice, muffled.

"I'm looking for Adrina Elkins." That was the name Ferron had given him. "I'm Lieutenant Haney. I have a bench warrant for her from traffic court. Failure to appear." He took

Larry Black's sheet from his pocket, the pages folded length-
wise, held it in front of the spyhole for a moment, then put it
away again.

"Traffic court?"

"That's what I said. Thirty-sixth District, City of Detroit.
It's signed by Judge Rogers. Adrina needs to come out and
talk to me."

"She's not here."

"Open the door."

"You got some ID?"

"You want to see my badge, open this door. You're starting to piss me off. Stop screwing around."

"She isn't here."

"Then open the door, prove it to me."

"Hold your badge up where I can see it."

"Open the fucking door. I'm not having a conversation
standing out here."

More silence, then, "If I let you in and you see she isn't
here, what then?"

"Then I leave this warrant with you and go home."

"Slide it under the door."

"You're wasting my time here, partner. The longer you make
me wait, the tougher things are going to be for Adrina when I
find her. You want her to spend a couple nights in County? I
can arrange it."

Silence, whoever was inside making a decision.

"Hold on." Locks being undone, a chain sliding out of its
guide. The door opened six inches, and Cordell King looked

out. Older than his booking photo, but the same man. Gold-frame glasses, jeans and tie-dyed T-shirt.

Burke grinned, stepped back, and heel-kicked the door at waist height. The edge cracked into Cordell's forehead, drove him back. He stumbled, fell into a sitting position, and then Burke was inside. He pushed the door shut behind him, drew the Browning. Cordell tried to stand, and Burke kicked him in the chest, knocked him back, his glasses flying off. Burke knelt, grabbed his T-shirt, twisted it tight, socketed the muzzle of the Browning behind his right ear, pressed hard. "Give me a reason."

Cordell stretched his arms out to the sides, showing he was unarmed. "Don't!"

"Anyone else in here?"

"What?"

He screwed the muzzle into Cordell's skin. "Is there anyone else in this apartment?"

"No."

"Lie there. Don't move."

Burke put the Browning away, got out a pair of flexcuffs, bent Cordell's arms behind him so he was facedown on the carpet, bound his wrists. He patted him down for weapons, found none, then took out the Browning again. When he stood, he was out of breath.

He looked around the living room. A couch and coffee table, big-screen TV. A bubbling tank against one wall, bright tropical fish inside, the water lit with a blue-green glow. A corridor ran the length of the apartment to a closed door.

"Stay there," Burke said. He went down the hallway. Kitchen, bathroom, bedroom at the end. It was empty. A sliding glass door there gave onto a small redwood deck.

He went back into the living room. "You are one stupid son of a bitch, you know that?"

Cordell didn't answer. His left cheek was pressed against the carpet.

"Where did your girlfriend go?" Burke said. "When's she coming back?"

"I don't know."

Burke knelt beside him, said, "Not too soon, I hope. Because if she comes walking through that door in the next few minutes, I'm going to shoot her in the head. How's that sound?"

Cordell twisted to look at him.

"Try again," Burke said. "When's she coming back?"

"I'm not sure. An hour maybe. Maybe less."

"Bad news for her if it's less."

He searched the apartment. On the floor of the bedroom closet was a black tactical bag. He dragged it out, unzipped it. Inside were banded packs of money, two automatics, a pistol-grip shotgun, and boxes of shells. The money was in thousand-dollar packs, but there were only eight of them. He took one of the packs, went back into the living room.

"Sit up," he said. Cordell didn't move. Burke gripped the flexcuffs, dragged him into a seated position. He knelt, slapped him lightly on the head with the money. "There better be more than eight thousand around here. For both your sakes."

"It's all I've got."

"You're as bad a liar as you were a thief, Cordell." He stood.

"If you make me rip this place apart, your shorty will probably come home while I'm doing it. How do you think that will end?"

Cordell let out his breath, looked at the floor.

"Time to give it up," Burke said. "You know what I'm talking about."

"It isn't here."

"Where is it?"

"Storage unit. In the city."

"There we go," Burke said. "That's a start." He got Cordell's glasses from the floor. There was a hairline crack at the bottom of the right lens. He fit them onto Cordell's face, pushed them up into place. "That better?"

Cordell made faces to get the glasses into position. He looked at Burke. "You work for Marquis?"

"Who's that?"

Burke went into the bedroom, put the money back in the tac bag, zipped it shut. He pulled a North Face coat off a hanger, carried both into the living room.

"How'd you find me?" Cordell said.

Burke took Ferron's license from his shirt pocket, dropped it in his lap. "That's cold, leaving a partner behind like that. Boy was in bad shape when I found him."

"What did you do?"

"I helped him out. We had a good long talk, too. So don't try to feed me any bullshit. I'll know it's bullshit, and I'm not in the mood. Can you stand up?"

"I don't think so."

"Come on, you can do it."

Burke took his arm, lifted until he could get his feet under him and stand. He swayed, and Burke steadied him.

"You got a lot of stones, kid. Ripping off Marquis Johnson, not trying to run afterward. I don't know if you're brilliant or stupid. You tell me."

He fit the coat over Cordell's shoulders, hiding the flex-cuffs.

"You know what happens now, right? We go find the rest of that money you stole. And if we don't, or you give me some sort of runaround, I'll pop you, then come back and pop that sweet piece of tail you call a girlfriend. You believe me?"

Cordell nodded.

"Good," Burke said. He picked up the tac bag, gave Cordell a push toward the door. "Let's take a ride."

In the car, Cordell was silent. He looked out the window, watching the buildings go by. He was done.

"Don't look so down," Burke said. "You may come out of all this okay after all."

"We were supposed to go to Cali."

"How's that?" They were on Eight Mile, headed to the address Cordell had given him. It was almost dark.

"Kevin had a brother in L.A.," Cordell said. "We were going to lay back there afterward, figure out what to do next."

"What happened?"

"When Kevin got shot, that changed everything. He's the one had it all set up. I didn't even know the man."

"You're lucky," Burke said. "Lucky it was me found you first, and not Marquis or Damien. If they'd caught up with you, they'd have killed you and your girlfriend both, just on general principles. You smoke?"

Cordell looked at him. Burke took the Newports from his coat pocket.

"Sometimes," Cordell said.

"How about now?"

Cordell nodded.

"Lean forward. To your right." Steering one-handed, Burke slipped the jacket off Cordell's shoulders, then took the scarab cutter from his coat pocket, opened it. "A little more." Cordell hunched, and Burke fit the blade on the flexcuffs, sliced through.

"Move those arms around," Burke said. "Get the circulation back." He closed the cutter, put it away

Cordell brought his arms around front, rolled his shoulders.

"Sorry I had to do that," Burke said. "But I couldn't take the risk, you know? Bad-ass like you, who knows what could have happened."

He tossed the pack of Newports on the dash. Cordell rubbed his wrists, took the pack, and shook one out. Burke gave him his lighter.

"Couple things you need to face, Cordell. This big adventure you had, it's over. You're still alive, and you got your baby mama, or whatever she is, back there. You came out ahead. But that money you took, you can't keep it. You need to accept that."

Cordell got the cigarette lit, coughed. Burke took his lighter back, dropped it in a pocket.

"Your buddy Kevin told me you walked out of that house with nearly two hundred K."

Cordell shook his head. "Wasn't that much. Those other two got most of it."

"Which two?"

"Woman and the white man."

Burke took the folded papers from his pocket, smoothed them on his thigh, held them out. "Look at that photo. That him?"

Cordell took the papers, nodded. "He and the woman got away."

"He didn't get far. One of you tagged him good. They found his body around the corner. Tell me more about the woman." Trying to keep the kid calm, talking.

"Charlie brought her in."

"That your cousin? One that got burned up in the house?"

"Yeah. He'd worked with her before. The white man, too. He knew her from way back."

"What's her name?"

"They called her Crissa. Never heard a last name."

"Where's she from?"

"Don't know."

"Hard to believe, a woman running with a crew of hard-core stickup boys like that. She and Black come out here together?"

"I think. Yeah."

Partners, then, Burke thought.

"So you took what, three twenty-five K, something like that, out of that drop car, right? Split it in half?"

Cordell nodded, drew in smoke, coughed again.

"And this Crissa got away with one-eighty of that?"

"Their split."

"And you stashed the rest? Kevin didn't get a piece?"

"Wasn't time. He didn't seem too bad at first, he was walking around okay. Looked like it went right through. I patched him up best I could, but he kept getting worse. Couldn't bring him to no hospital."

"You leave him that black tar?"

"Yeah, went out and copped it. Least I could do." He looked at Burke. "He dead?"

Burke nodded. Cordell looked away, blinked. His eyes were shiny.

"Man up, son," Burke said. "You wanted to play with the big dogs. This is no time to start acting like a bitch. This where we turn off?" A sign ahead said SOUTHFIELD FREEWAY.

"Yeah."

"Tell me something else," Burke said. "About this Crissa."

"What?"

"When things started to jump off back at the house, everybody shooting, she get hit?"

"I don't think so. She moved too fast. Shoulda had her right there, but she went out the window. Kevin tried to get her, but he's the one got shot instead. Bitch was fierce."

"I'm not surprised."

"What you mean?"

"You ever hear what they tell commandos, the antiterrorist

teams, Navy SEALs? Kind that go into a situation, rescue hostages, blow the bad guys' shit up?"

Cordell shook his head.

"Thing is, in those terrorist groups, the women are the real hard cases. It's the same with gangbangers, right? You don't mess with the women." He took the cigarettes from the dash, got one out, speared his lips, used his lighter. "So when they're training these counterterror teams, they tell them when they're going into a situation where there's multiple targets—men and women—you shoot the women first."

"Why?"

He blew out smoke. "Because in a gang or a crew or what-ever, a woman's got to be three times as tough, three times as committed, three times as hard-ass for the men to take her seriously. And a man'll naturally hesitate if he's pointing a gun at a woman. Long enough to get shot himself. That's why they tell them take out the women first, even the odds."

"I never heard that."

"It's true. That's what you should have done in that house. Would have saved you a lot of time and trouble. Look where you are now, because of her."

"She fucked things up for sure."

"No, *you* fucked things up. She was the professional, you two were the amateurs. This shit ain't a game. Not everyone's made for it."

He followed Cordell's directions to where the freeway turned into Southfield Road. The storage facility was the only light on a dark block, a small city of low flat buildings. He slowed as they neared the entrance.

Cordell's cigarette was done. He powered down the passenger window, dropped the butt out.

"You know, I'm not like Marquis, or Damien," Burke said. "I don't have anything against anybody. All I want is the jack."

"Then what?"

"Then I'm going to haul ass out of this town. I've done some things you can't undo, you know? Time to start over somewhere. What you should be doing, too. How much you need?"

"What?"

"You've got to run. You understand that, right? You don't have a choice. If Damien catches up with you, he'll cut off those big balls of yours, feed them to you before he puts a bullet in your head. How much for you and Adrina, get out of Detroit, go somewhere he can't find you?"

Cordell looked at him, didn't answer.

"I've done some bad shit last couple days," Burke said. "Things I'm not proud of. Don't want to do anymore if I can avoid it. Now I know what you're thinking. You're thinking, a couple hours ago, all that money belonged to you. And now it doesn't. But you need to concentrate on tomorrow, not yesterday. Will twenty thousand do it?"

"You serious?"

"Why not? Twenty's better than nothing, right? Anyway, you earned it, all the shit you went through. And if there's as much as you say in there, there's plenty to go around."

He pulled up to the gate, used the key card Cordell had given him. When the gate swung open, he drove through.

"Left here," Cordell said. "It's down about halfway on the right."

Burke drove slow, no other cars around. The units they were driving past now were all garage-size, the narrow streets brightly lit.

"That's it there," Cordell said.

Burke pulled up, put his headlights on the orange metal door. It was padlocked to a small U-bolt in the concrete.

Burke switched off the headlights, killed the engine. He took the Browning from his coat pocket. "Any surprises in there and you'll go down first."

"Won't be no surprises."

"Good. Get your key."

They got out of the car together. Cordell was moving slow. He undid the padlock, slipped it free of the bolt, pushed the door up on its rollers. Inside was a silver Lexus, parked nose first against the far wall.

"You first," Burke said. He tossed his cigarette away.

Cordell went in, hit a wall switch. Fluorescent ceiling bulbs blinked on. Burke came in behind him, used his left hand to pull the door back down until it met the concrete lip of the entrance.

"It's in the trunk," Cordell said.

Burke gestured with the Browning. "Open it."

Cordell took out a key fob, pressed a button, and the trunk lid clicked, opened an inch. He raised it the rest of the way.

"Step back," Burke said. "Go stand over there."

He did as he was told. Burke looked in the trunk. Inside were two more black tac bags. He unzipped one, saw banded

packs of cash jumbled together. In the second were handguns, extra magazines, and two Kevlar vests. He could see the
parts of a disassembled AR-15.

"Start a war with this shit," he said. "You people were
prepared, give you that." He put the Browning in his coat
pocket, hauled out the bag with the money, propped it on
the fender, tilted it to get a better look at the bills. "This the
rest of it?"

"That's it."

"No one else touched it?"

"No."

"You didn't stash any someplace else, just in case?"

"Wasn't time."

"So there should be about a hundred and fifty thousand
in here, that what you're telling me?"

"'Bout that." He was rubbing his wrists again.

"Pretty big score for a guy your age. And hell, you almost
got away with it." He dropped the bag on the floor. "Count
that shit for me."

Cordell pushed his glasses up on his nose, knelt, and opened
the bag wider. He began to take out bound packs, set them
on the concrete floor. Burke leaned back against the Lexus's
fender, crossed his arms.

"Rough count's good enough," he said. "Doesn't have to
be to the dollar."

Cordell nodded, counting out packs, lips moving silently.

"When you're done, don't forget to take out your twenty,"
Burke said. "That's twenty. Not thirty, not forty. I'm watching you."

Cordell moved stacks to one side, took more from the bag.

"Count it twice," Burke said, "just to be sure," then took the slapjack from his coat pocket, raised it high, and laid it across the back of Cordell's head. He grunted, fell forward across the money, and Burke leaned over, hit him again, then a third time.

He rolled him off the money, grabbed his belt, dragged him clear, turned him faceup. He was still breathing. Burke used the slapjack on him four more times. When he was done, there was blood on the leather. He wiped it on Cordell's T-shirt, then put the slapjack away.

The money went back into the tac bag. He zipped it up, then checked the rest of the car. There was blood on the passenger seat. That would be Ferron's. No other cash.

He went back to Cordell, wrestled him closer to the car, then gripped his belt, lifted. He got his head and shoulders inside the trunk, then raised his legs, tumbled him inside atop the other bag. His glasses were on the floor a few feet away. Burke threw them in after him, shut the lid.

Out of breath, he opened the gate, looked out on the street. Still empty. He stowed the tac bag in the Impala's trunk beside the other one, then switched off the lights inside the unit, rolled the door shut, and padlocked it again.

He used the key card at the gate, headed back toward the freeway. He lit another cigarette, threw the padlock key out the window. A mile later, he tossed the key card.

Time for a road trip, he thought. If it worked out, he'd come back here, get the rest of his money from the bank and what he'd hidden in the house. Then head out, someplace far away, worry about Marquis later. Or maybe pay a quick visit to Terry Street first, take out Marquis and his brother both, never have to worry about either of them again.

Time to finish this shit up, he thought, find the woman, find the money.

Just you and me now, honey, he thought. Let's see what you got.

NINETEEN

They'd been on the road more than an hour, Claudette in the backseat, Haley sleeping in her lap. Crissa looked at them in the rearview, said, "Are you awake?" They were on Interstate 95 now, heading north.

Claudette raised her head, blinked. She'd been drifting in and out of sleep the last twenty miles. "Yes."

"How do you feel about what happened back there?"

"What do you mean?"

"We need to talk some things out, and we need to be on the same page with it."

Haley shifted in her sleep.

"How much does he know about your sister?" Crissa said.

"Not much. Her name. Town she lives in. That's about it."

"We need a plan, in case he comes looking for you."

"He won't."

"He might. So you have to plan as if he will. But you know what the biggest danger is?" She caught Claudette's eyes in the mirror.

"What?"

"You decide you miss him, try to go back."

Claudette looked out the window. "I don't think I could do that. Not now. Not after today."

"Good."

"I feel bad for him, though."

"Don't."

"Sometimes you see things, know things," Claudette said. "But you ignore them, hope they'll go away on their own, that things'll get better."

"Sometimes they do. Mostly they don't."

"I know."

"Anyway, if Roy's smart, he's on his way to Alaska right now."

"He can be," Claudette said. "Sometimes."

"What?"

"Smart."

"Let's hope," Crissa said.

It was just before 2:00 A.M. when she steered the rental into the gravel driveway. It was lined with live oaks on one side. Spanish moss hung from the branches, gray and ghostly in the headlights.

The house was set back from the road, the homes here spaced out, separated by undeveloped lots. Lights on the porch and in the front room. She parked behind a dark red SUV, shut off the headlights and engine.

The front door opened, and a woman came out on the porch.

"Go talk to her," Crissa said. "I'll get your things."

Claudette got the door open, slid across and out. She lifted Haley up to her shoulder. They started across the yard to the porch and the woman waiting there.

Crissa got out, stretched, touched her toes to ease her back muscles. The air was thick and smelled of nearby swamp, a faint sulfur scent in the air. The night was full of crickets. She thought of her own house, the smell of the inlet, the far-off sound of the channel buoys at night. The noise of the wind, the echo of empty rooms.

She opened the trunk, got out the black trash bag and the single suitcase. Roy had kept the other one. She carried them up the lawn to the slate path that led to the door, the bag slung over her shoulder. Claudette and the woman had stopped talking, were looking back at her.

Crissa tried to smile despite her fatigue, set the suitcase down, said, "Hello." The woman standing next to Claudette was in her early forties, blond hair tied back. Crissa could see the resemblance in the eyes, the facial features.

"This is Crissa," Claudette said. "Crissa, my sister Nancy. This is her house."

Haley made a noise in her sleep, her head on Claudette's shoulder.

"Let me take her," Nancy said. "I've got the downstairs

bedroom made up already." Claudette shifted Haley into her sister's arms. Without opening her eyes, Haley put her arms around Nancy's neck, her head on her shoulder. Nancy shifted her for a better grip, looked at Crissa.

"And what are you again?"

"Just a friend," Crissa said.

"Well, y'all better come in, then," Nancy said. "I guess we have some talking to do."

"Do you have any idea," Nancy said, "how many times I've been through this?"

She and Crissa sat in the living room, a single light on. Claudette was asleep beside Haley in the spare bedroom.

"I can imagine," Crissa said, and sipped from her mug of herbal tea. It was a big living room, with a sloped ceiling and skylight, a brick fireplace. An old house, but plenty of space, and it would be full of light in the daytime.

"From the time she was fifteen," Nancy said. "One thing after another. One man after another. With Larry, and then Haley, I thought she'd settle down. At least it seemed that way for a while. But I guess he had his issues, too."

"He did."

"But he's not coming back, is he?"

"No."

"He paid for Claudette's rehab last time. Not long after she had Haley. He was a good provider when he was around. You think she's done with that Roy?"

"Maybe. Until the next time she gets high, decides he wasn't such a bad guy after all."

"Will he come after her? Will he come here?"

"I doubt it, but you never know. He doesn't have a car, but that doesn't mean he can't get access to one. If it's all right with you, I'd like to stick around here a couple days, just in case."

"And what would you do if he does?"

"I don't know. I'll deal with it if it happens," Crissa said. "Anyway, I imagine he'd call first, ask her to come back. If that's what he wants. But who knows what he's thinking? He's a junkie, using junkie logic. He sees himself as the victim in all this."

She drank her tea. "This is a beautiful house."

"Thanks. Michael and I bought it right after we got married. It was bigger than we needed, but we figured we'd have kids before long, you know? Turns out I couldn't. Took me a long time to find out, though. We were looking into adopting just before Michael got sick. And after that . . . well, there was no after that."

"I'm sorry."

"I can't say I was happy to get that phone call tonight. But at least Claudette's here, and alive. I won't have to worry so much about her and Haley now. I can take care of both of them, for a while at least."

Crissa set her mug on the coffee table. "Take a walk with me. I want to show you something."

They went outside. Mist lay ankle-deep on the ground. Crissa opened the trunk of the rental. On the way up here, she'd stopped at a convenience store, bought a cheap nylon sports bag, transferred the money into it.

"What am I looking at?" Nancy said.

Crissa unzipped the bag, opened it, took out her penlight, and shone the beam inside.

"What is this?" Nancy said.

"Seventy-three thousand dollars, more or less. It belonged to Larry. I had to spend some of it."

Nancy was silent for a moment, then said, "Am I not supposed to ask how he got it?"

"Gambling," Crissa said.

"I didn't know Larry was a gambler."

"In his way. But there's nothing to worry about. It's all clean. No one's going to come looking for it. It belongs to Claudette and Haley."

"Does Claudette know about this?"

"She knows there's money. She doesn't know how much. And I'm not going to tell her. I'm leaving it with you."

Nancy looked at her. "And why would you do that?"

"Like I said, it's for Claudette and Haley. And you're the best person to decide how it should be used."

"You trust me that much? We just met."

"I don't have any choice, do I?" Crissa said.

"Let's go back inside. I think I need a drink. Something a little stronger than tea."

"That," Crissa said, "sounds like a good idea."

* * *

She woke on the couch with a start, not knowing where she was. The comforter Nancy had given her slipped off, fell to the floor. She was fully dressed, had fallen asleep almost as soon as she'd lain down.

She sat up. Haley stood a few feet away, watching her. She wore Minnie Mouse pajamas, carried the stuffed squirrel.

"Hey," Crissa said. "What are you doing up?" Dawn was a pale glow in the living room window.

"I was scared."

"Of what?"

"That you'd left. Without saying good-bye."

"I wouldn't do that."

"Daddy did."

"Come here."

Haley stepped forward, and Crissa took her in her arms, squeezed her for a moment, then let go. "I'd never leave you like that. How's Sammy the squirrel holding up there?"

"That's not his name."

"What is?"

"He doesn't have a name. He's a squirrel."

"He looks sleepy," Crissa said. "You should both go back to bed. It's early."

"I was worried."

"Don't be," Crissa said. "I'm not going anywhere."

Crissa unzipped the sports bag on the table, opened it. Sunlight streamed in through the big kitchen windows. The backyard ran down to a small stream, with woods beyond.

Claudette and Haley were walking along the creekside, picking up stones and examining them, looking for arrowheads. Every few steps, Haley would crouch, look intently into the water as if watching something below the surface.

"All that money looks different in the daylight," Nancy said.

"You have a safe in the house?"

"No."

"Then your best bet's a safe deposit box at a bank. Take what you need as you need it. Leave the rest where no one can get at it besides you."

"Can't I just deposit it in an account?"

"Not unless you want the IRS knocking on your door the next day. Banks have to report every cash deposit of ten thousand dollars or over. If you do make deposits, keep them lower than that, and not too frequent. Even better if you spread it out into smaller accounts, CDs, money market funds, whatever."

"You sound like you've had some experience with this."

"A little."

"I've never seen this much money at once in my entire life."

"It goes faster than you'd imagine. I have something else for you, too."

She took a cell phone from the bag, set it on the table.

"What's that?" Nancy said.

"A disposable. For emergencies. There's only one number in it. This one." She took out a second phone, identical to the first. She'd bought both on the drive there. "After I leave, you need to reach me, or anything happens—she hears from Roy, whatever—you call me. You'll be the only one with this number. So if it rings, I'll know it's you. Show Claudette and Haley, too, just in case."

"I will."

Crissa zipped the bag shut again, hefted it. "Where can we put this for now?"

"My room's best. Upstairs. There's a panel in the ceiling of the closet there. I'll show you. Is it heavy?"

"Heavier than you'd think," Crissa said.

She stood at the kitchen window, watched the sun setting over the woods. Claudette was at the sink, doing the rest of the dinner dishes. After they'd eaten, Nancy had left for her night shift at the hospital. Haley was in the living room, stretched out on the carpet, watching television.

"You really think he'll come?" Claudette said. She was drying her hands with a dish towel.

"I don't know. Maybe. Or maybe he'll just call, try to get you to go back to him."

"I needed to get away from him, from that life. I knew that. But it's hard sometimes, you know? You get used to things. It's like you say you'll never become a certain type of person. And then one day you wake up, and that's who you are. And you're not sure how it happened."

"I'll stay here another day, just in case," Crissa said. "Then head home."

"Where do you live?"

"Up north."

"You don't give much away, do you?"

"You'll need to find a school for Haley here. The sooner the better."

"I know. And I need to thank you. For everything you've done."

Crissa locked the back door, touched the light switch beside it. The yard lit up all the way to the woods.

"Let me tell you something," she said. "From experience. The tough part hasn't started yet. You'll be in a strange environment, doing unfamiliar things, and doing them clean. It's like you said, you'll want to go back to what you know, what's comfortable, even if it's killing you. That's the way it works."

"I don't think I could ever go back," Claudette said. "Not after what's happened."

"You caught some bad breaks along the way," Crissa said. "But it doesn't have to be that way for Haley. She has a chance. Don't fuck it up for her."

"This isn't all my fault, you know, everything's that happened."

"No one said it was."

Crissa went out to the living room. Haley was still on the floor, crayons and coloring book spread out in front of her, the television blaring. Crissa stood in the doorway, looked down at her.

She's not yours, she thought. And she's never going to be. She's got her own family, her own life, and you're no part of either. You're stalling, because you don't want to go back to an empty house, and a town full of strangers.

Claudette came into the living room. She sat beside Haley

on the floor, said, "Hey, sweetie. How you making out with that?"

Haley slid over to make room for her. Neither of them looked up as Crissa walked past them, out the front door and into the dark.

TWENTY

Burke parked at the curb, looked at the house. It was the right address, the one he'd gotten from Black's rap sheet. He read the notice on the door, said, "Son of a bitch."

All this way and no one here. It had taken him a day and a half to drive to Florida. He'd stopped in Kentucky the night before, then driven the rest in one shot. He'd left the Impala in a parking garage in Orlando, rented the Buick from a local agency, not wanting his Michigan plates to attract attention. He'd transferred the two tac bags to the trunk.

It was almost dusk. He got out, went up to the door, rang the bell, heard it echo inside. He tried the knob. Locked. The window, too. He went around back, and the door and windows there were boarded. But the plywood on one window hung loose at an angle. He slid it aside, saw a dark empty room inside, trash on the floor, a bare mattress and a camping lantern, a crack pipe. The room smelled of sweat and pot smoke.

He let the plywood swing back, saw the two nails on the ground. He picked them up. The heads were weathered, but the shafts shiny. It hadn't been long since they'd been pried loose from the wood.

He went back to the car. He'd go find a room somewhere, get something to eat, come back later, see if anyone showed up. It wasn't much to go on, but he'd come this far. He'd play the cards he was dealt.

At nine o'clock, he was back at the house, watching from across the street. The ashtray was full. He'd slept an hour, eaten, and felt better now. It was too warm for the coat he'd brought, so he'd bought a zippered jacket at a store nearby.

At first he thought it was just fatigue, his eyes playing tricks on him. A glow of light in the dark window of the house, bright for a moment, then dimmer.

He lit another cigarette, saw a shadow pass by the window, someone moving around inside there.

He got the Browning from under the seat, tucked it into his belt, zipped the jacket up over it, pulled on his gloves.

He'd wait, let them get their smoke on in there, if that's what they were doing. He finished his cigarette, then got out of the car, went up the side yard of the house. He could hear TV noise from an open window of the house next door, caught a glimpse of a living room, a gray-haired woman eating a bowl of ice cream, intent on what she was watching, not noticing him as he went by.

The plywood still hung loose. He could hear whispers inside, the hiss and sizzle of a pipe. The lantern was on low, lighting up the floor and the man and woman sitting on the edge of the mattress. He had a ponytail, wore a torn flannel shirt with the sleeves buttoned. The woman was thin and blond, in a dirty tank top and cutoff jeans. When the man handed her the crack pipe, Burke saw the star tattoo on the side of his neck. She fired the bowl with a plastic lighter, drew on the pipe.

He took out the Browning, wanting to get this over with, find out what he could and move on. With his other hand, he pulled back the plywood, heard it crack. It swung free, and the two inside looked up. He pointed the gun at them, said, "Police. Don't move."

The woman dropped the pipe.

"Up," Burke said.

The man stood slowly, unsteady on his feet. He raised his hands. "It's cool, man. It's okay. I used to live here."

The woman stood, too, looked at the doorway.

"No, really, it's cool," the man said. "We didn't break in. This was my house."

"That so?" Burke said, keeping the gun on him. He looked at the woman. "What about you?"

"I just came here to party."

"Get out." When she didn't move, he nodded at the doorway. "I said go on, get out of here."

She looked at him, then bolted from the room. He heard her fumbling at the front door.

"What's your name?" Burke said.

"Roy."

"Roy what?"

"Mapes."

"You say you used to live here?"

"Yeah, man. This was my house."

"Come out here, Roy," Burke said, "and talk to me."

They were sitting at a table outside a fast-food restaurant, Mapes working on his second hot dog. Burke had sent him to the counter with a twenty-dollar bill, told him to get what he wanted. Now Burke smoked and watched him eat.

"What they did," Mapes said when he was finished. "It wasn't right."

"No," Burke said. He'd heard most of the story on the way here. "You deserved better than that."

"You're goddamn right. Can I get one of those?"

Burke put the pack in front of him.

"You scared the shit out of me back there," Mapes said. "When I saw that gun, I thought it was all over."

"Sorry about that. Can't be too careful, right? You want another coney?"

"A what?"

"A hot dog."

Mapes shook his head. "I'm good."

"So you have no place to go now?"

"Can't go back to the motel. Don't have enough money to go somewhere else. That bitch fucked up everything for me."

"Maybe we can do something about that."

"What's that mean?"

"This woman you're talking about. I think she's the one I've been looking for."

"Why?"

Burke didn't answer.

"That's okay," Mapes said. "None of my business, right?"

Burke took a fifty-dollar bill from his pocket, folded it and stuck it under the paper plate. "That's for your trouble."

Mapes looked at it, then at him.

"Go ahead," Burke said. "Take it."

Mapes slid it off the table, put it in his shirt pocket.

"Tell me," Burke said. "You ever see this money they were always talking about?"

Mapes shook his head. "She had it someplace else. I don't know where."

"And she took it with her when they left? All of it?"

"That's what pissed me off. They could've left something for me, right?"

"Should have, definitely. You get a sense how much there was?"

"No, but it was a lot. She had plenty with her to spend."

Burke watched a stray dog trot through the parking lot, sniff at an overstuffed trash can.

"You ever hear a last name?" Burke said.

"Just Crissa. That's all. Maybe she told Claudette her last name, but I never heard it."

Maybe not such a pro after all, Burke thought. Hanging around, telling people she had money for them, when she should be holed up someplace, spending it. It didn't make any sense.

There was a fading bruise on Mapes's cheek. Burke touched his own face in the same place, said, "She do that to you?"

"No way, man. If she'd tried to touch me, I'd have beat her ass good."

"You sure about that?"

"I don't ever let a woman put her hands on me."

"She really got to you, huh?"

"I was taking care of shit. I had things all worked out, a plan. And she fucked it all up."

Mapes sat back abruptly, arms crossed, let out smoke, looked away.

Burke slid the pack toward him. "Keep them."

"You sure?"

"Go ahead."

He put them in his shirt pocket. "Why you looking for her?"

"I have my reasons."

"You a friend of hers?"

"Not by a long shot."

"Somebody needs to set her straight, you know what I mean?"

"I do. Exactly. Can you help me do that?"

Mapes sniffed. "I don't know. Maybe."

"There'd be more money, if you're interested," Burke said. "Maybe a lot."

"Whose money?"

"Who do you think?"

"That money belonged to me as much as Claudette."

"Good reason why we should find it, then. You might end up with a piece of it after all."

"How?"

"She's got it. I want it. You help me find it, you'll get a share."

"How much?"

"Depends how much you help, doesn't it? And how much we find. But it'll be enough to set you up for a while. You can find a decent place to live, not that rathole vacant back there. Get some new clothes, clean yourself up."

"Get organized."

"That's right."

"What do I have to do?"

"You know where they went, right? When they left here?"

"Yeah, I do."

"Then there you go. Tell me."

"I'll do better than that," Mapes said. "I'll take you there."

Driving north on I-95, Burke watched thunderclouds gather on the horizon. Dark gray at first, then turning black, lightning pulsing inside.

"Gonna storm," Mapes said.

Burke shifted in his seat. He was tired, but the adrenaline was keeping him going. Mapes had talked nonstop for the first hour in the car, Burke nodding, but hardly listening.

Every once in a while he'd shut up, and Burke would look over to see him nodding out. Then his eyes would spring open, and he'd start talking again as if there'd been no break.

It started raining when they passed Daytona, thick drops that spotted the windshield. He watched for signs. He'd turn off on U.S. 1, take it north up along the coast, find a place for both of them to stay that night. He wanted to be awake and alert when he reached St. Augustine.

He rolled his neck to ease the stiffness. He needed coffee and a night's sleep, but there would be time enough to rest soon. He was closer than he'd ever been before, to the woman, to the money. Before tomorrow night, he might find both.

Mapes began to snore. Burke looked at him. His head was against the passenger window, eyes closed.

Thunder boomed above them. Mapes snorted, didn't wake. Burke made a pistol with his right hand, touched the index finger to Mapes's left temple, said, softly, "Pow."

He didn't stir. Burke took his hand away, drove on under the black sky.

TWENTY-ONE

On her third day there, Crissa took Haley into town, found a Target, let her pick out school supplies. She was mostly silent while they shopped, but she held Crissa's hand without protest. At the register, Crissa bought her a Mylar balloon with Minnie Mouse on it.

Driving home, the balloon bobbing in the backseat, they passed a park on the edge of town, saw a petting zoo set up inside a fenced-in area.

"Horses," Haley said, and pointed.

"They sure are," Crissa said. "Let's go say hello."

She slowed, turned down a side street and into the entrance to the parking lot. Haley was unbuckling herself before the car came to a stop. "Easy, angel," Crissa said. "Wait for me."

Inside the fenced area were two ponies, a pair of potbellied pigs, and three sheep, all in separate pens, attended by teen-agers. Four-H'ers, Crissa guessed. The five-dollar admission benefited a local children's hospital. Crissa paid for Haley, then slipped a fifty into the donation jar on the folding table.

There were food carts and benches underneath an oak tree, Spanish moss hanging down. Crissa sat, watched a teenage girl lift Haley onto a long-haired Shetland pony, lead her slowly around the pen. She was scared at first, clung tight to the saddle horn, but by the second circuit she was grinning. She looked back at Crissa and waved, then leaned forward to stroke the pony's hair.

Leave tomorrow, Crissa thought. Return the car, catch the train back north. The longer you stay, the harder it'll be to leave, for both of you. In time, with luck, Haley might forget what had happened, start a new life here.

But she felt no rush to get back. There was nothing wait-ing for her there, nothing she needed to do. Maybe it was time to go away, someplace warm, like Jimmy had said. Do a little forgetting of her own.

The sky was red in the west, the sun sinking behind trees. The air smelled of cotton candy and popcorn. A shift in the breeze brought the scent of night-blooming jasmine. She closed her eyes.

When she opened them again, one of the teenagers was leading Haley out by the hand. She was laughing, Crissa re-alizing then it was the first time she'd ever seen that.

Crissa stood. "You have fun?" she said. "Ready to go home?"

Haley nodded, ran toward her. Crissa swept her up in her arms and carried her back to the car.

It was almost dark by the time they got to the house. Nancy's SUV was still in the driveway. She hadn't left for the hospital yet, must be running late. Crissa pulled alongside it so as not to block her in.

She shut off the engine, and Haley undid her harness, reached into the backseat for the balloon.

"Hold on to that tight," Crissa said. "Don't let it get away."

Crissa went around and opened the trunk, got out the red and white Target bag. Haley ran toward the house, the balloon streaming behind her. The front door opened, and she disappeared inside.

She shut the trunk, carried the bag across the lawn, and up onto the porch. The door was ajar. She shouldered it open, went in, and there was Roy, standing in the middle of the living room, holding a gun, Claudette and Nancy on the couch behind him.

Haley stood in front of him, empty-handed. The balloon was on the ceiling.

Crissa dropped the bag, stepped toward him, felt cold metal against the back of her neck.

"Easy there," a voice said behind her. "Just stay calm. I've been waiting a long time to meet you."

Claudette put out her arms, said, "Come here, sweetie." Crissa could see the fear in her eyes.

Haley looked back at Crissa.

"Go on," she said.

Haley went quickly around Roy, into her mother's arms. Claudette hugged her, tears streaming freely down her face now. Nancy was watching Roy, anger in her eyes.

"Step forward," the voice said. "Slow. I don't want this thing going off by accident. That's something nobody'll forget anytime soon."

She took a step, half-turned. The man behind her held a pistol-grip shotgun. He was in his forties maybe, dark hair combed back, black nylon jacket.

"Who are you?" she said.

He took a pair of flexcuffs from a jacket pocket, tossed them on the floor, said to Roy, "Take those two in the other room, the girl, too. There's only two cuffs, but you can handle a six-year-old, right?"

Roy sniffed, looked at Crissa. "I want to talk to her."

"Later," the man said. "Go on, take the others. Keep them quiet."

Roy moved to stand in front of her. His eyes were sunken, the pupils dilated.

"All that money go up your nose?" she said, and he leaned forward, spit in her face. She hit him without thinking, drove the heel of her right hand into his nose. It snapped his head back, sent him stumbling. The man behind her said, "Hello!"

Roy raised the gun, and the man aimed the shotgun at him and said, "Take a deep breath, boy. Later for that shit. Do what I say."

Roy glared at Crissa, touched his nose. A single drop of

blood came from the left nostril. "You shouldn't have done that."

"Go on," the man said to him. "What did I tell you about starting shit?"

Roy wiped the blood away, sniffed, bent and picked up the flexcuffs. He looked at Claudette said, "Get up. Let's go."

"No," she said. Haley's face was buried in her shoulder, eyes closed.

Roy pointed the gun at them, and Crissa saw now it was a Mini Glock.

"You should listen to me," he said, "You know, shit could get real ugly in here."

"Go on," Crissa said to her. "Nancy, you, too. Everything'll be okay. We're just going to talk." Wanting Haley out of the room if there was shooting.

"Listen to the woman," the man with the shotgun said.

"Come on," Roy said again, angry. Nancy stood, said, "Claudette, let's do what he says."

Claudette rose, Haley holding on tight. "Roy, why are you doing this to us?"

"Why did you do what you did to me? Get in there." He waved the gun at them.

"Stay with them," the man with the shotgun said. "Make sure there's no phones they can get at, anything like that. Go on."

Roy walked them into the downstairs bedroom. Crissa wiped the spit from her face. The shotgun muzzle flicked her ear. "Hands," the man said.

She raised her hands, and he put the muzzle under her

chin, bent her head back, patted her down with his free hand. It was thorough, professional, his hand never lingering too long in a single place.

When he was done, he nodded at the couch. "Sit."

Hands still up, she backed until she felt the edge of the couch against her legs. She sat.

He stepped back, the shotgun still on her. "You have any idea how far I've come, looking for you?"

"Who are you?"

"You asked me that already. Who am I? I'm the one that's come for the money you stole."

"What money?"

"That the way you're going to play it? Marquis's money. Did you think it was going to be that easy to keep it?"

She lowered her hands, watching him.

He dragged a chair over, sat, the shotgun across his knees, still angled at her. "You recognize this? I got it from your buddy Cordell."

She looked at it, saw it was the Mossberg 12-gauge she'd used in Detroit. And the Mini Glock Roy had would be hers as well, the one she'd dropped in the driveway when she and Larry had run from the house.

"He held on to it all this time," the man said. "Not sure why. Had a bag of guns and a bag of money in his girlfriend's apartment. Not the sharpest knife in the drawer, I'm thinking. But he did outsmart you and your partners, right? So you have to give him some credit."

"You work for Marquis?"

"People keep asking me that."

"What happened to this Cordell you're talking about?"

"What do you think?" The Mossberg shifted on his legs. "And just so you know, there's 12-gauge buck in here, double-oh. You try to get up and I'll take your leg off at the knee before your ass even leaves that cushion."

"You need that much gun for this?"

"Can't be too careful, all the shit I heard about you. Besides, man's gotta respect a shotgun, right? Woman, too. It cuts to the chase. It's that noise it makes when you rack it, lets people know you mean business."

He opened his coat to show her the butt of a gun in his belt. "Now, that's for up close and personal."

"I see."

"Anyone else you want to ask me about?"

"No."

"You sure? How about Ferron, the one you shot? You fucked him up good. Can't blame you, seeing what happened. Though it's still hard to believe a couple of numbnuts like that took down a crew of pros. Or at least I thought you were pros. Seeing you here now, I have to wonder. What are you doing here anyway? What was Black to you?"

"Does it matter?"

"Not much, I guess. I found you, that's what counts."

"If you don't work for Marquis, who do you work for?"

"Formerly for the Detroit Police Department. That was a while ago, though. My new profession pays a hell of a lot better, at least recently. I took a chunk of change off your friend

Cordell. He didn't have time to spend much of it. But I knew there was more out there somewhere. And that's how we've come to the place we are right now."

She nodded toward the other room. "And you trust him to help you with that?"

"He's something, isn't he? But he has his purpose. Doesn't like you much, I see. In fact, you just seem to piss people off everywhere you go."

He got a pack of Newports from his jacket pocket, shook one loose, got it between his lips. The other hand stayed on the shotgun. He put the cigarettes away, got out a lighter. "You want me to tell you how this is going to go?"

"How's that?"

He lit the cigarette. "You've got money, maybe as much as a hundred and sixty thousand, from what I hear. And you've probably got some of it with you. That's what you're doing here, right? Delivering your partner's share to his family? Admirable. But in this case, not too smart."

He put the lighter away, blew out smoke.

"Way it's going to go is, you're going to hand over that money to me. Or if it's not here in this house, you're going to take me where it is, while Shithead in there stays with the women. And if you give me the runaround, I make a call and he starts doing them one by one until I tell him to stop. The little girl, too."

"You think he's got the stones for that?"

"We'll find out. And when that collateral is used up, you get a chance to decide how much your own life is worth. Is it worth a hundred and sixty thousand?"

"There was never that much."

"Oh, no? Then how much was there?"

"It doesn't matter. You're not going to let any of us live anyway."

"That's where you're wrong. All I want is the jack. You think I want to be in here waving a shotgun around, scaring women and children? You think I want to be down here at all? I take your money and leave you alive, what are you going to do anyway? Call the cops? Come after me? That would be a foolish thing."

"I don't even know who you are."

"That's right. And better that way."

"Marquis will want his money back. Sooner or later he'll hear you found it."

"Fuck Marquis. He thinks he's some sort of criminal genius. He runs a few ghetto blocks in the most fucked-up city in the country. Marquis can do what he wants. He can't touch me."

Roy came out into the living room, the gun in his belt. "What's going on?"

"We're talking," the man said. "Go back in there."

"She tell you where the money is?"

"There won't be any money if one of them gets away, finds a phone. I told you, don't leave them alone."

Roy looked at Crissa. "Don't trust her."

"Go on back. Keep an eye on them. I'll come in in a few, let you know what the deal is."

Roy went back in. The man looked at her, said, "You've got some balls. But brains, too, I hope. Because all four of you can walk away from this like nothing happened. I might even let you keep a piece of that money yourself."

"I'm supposed to believe that?" she said.

"Believe what you like. But I've always considered myself a reasonable man. One of my virtues." He blew out smoke.

"Like I said, it was never a hundred and sixty."

"How much, then?"

She shifted in her seat. He moved the shotgun to cover her, his finger on the trigger.

"Larry's share was only half that," she said. "Eighty thousand. And some of that got spent already."

"What happened to your cut?"

"It's laundered and gone."

"I guess I expected that. So where's the other eighty?"

"I told you, it's less than that."

"Where is it?"

"Close by."

"There, see? Now we're getting someplace."

She nodded at the other room. "What about him?"

"He's got nothing to do with this."

"He thinks he does."

"He can think what he wants. This is between you and me."

Crissa looked down the hallway to the kitchen, the brightly lit yard beyond. No one at the back door. So maybe it was just the two of them, and there was a way to play them out of the house with no one getting hurt.

"What do you say?" the man said. "Comes down to it, way things are right now, you don't really have a lot of choices."

"I don't care about the money. I care about the little girl."

"Then that makes the choice simpler, right?"

"It's in the house, but you'll never find it on your own."

"Don't push me," he said. "Especially when we're just starting to make progress. I could kill all of you, then spend all night looking. I'd find it eventually."

"You might. You might not. And Nancy"—she lifted her chin toward the other room—"is a nurse. She was due at the hospital an hour ago. They'll call at some point, to check. And if they get no answer, they'll send someone out. So you may not have much time."

He frowned. "Shit's never easy with you, is it?"

"Get rid of him." She pointed at the other room. "And I'll get you the money." Wanting them separated. Better odds if an opportunity arose.

"What difference is it to you?" he said.

"Way I want it. I don't trust him around the girl."

He looked at her for a moment, dropped the cigarette on the carpet. He stood, the shotgun at port arms, ground the butt out with his heel, and said, "Mapes, get out here."

"What?"

"I said get out here."

Roy came out into the living room, the gun still in his belt. The man took keys from his jacket pocket, tossed them. Roy caught them in the air.

"Go get the car," the man said. "Bring it up the driveway."

"Why?"

"Because we're not staying long, and I'm not walking all the way back through those woods when we're done. Just do it. Leave the engine running."

Roy went out the front door. The breeze moved the balloon along the ceiling.

"I don't think he'd mind if you had a bullet in your head when we left here," the man said.

"He's not much of a partner for someone like you."

"He isn't. Now get the money."

"I want to check on them first."

"Forget it. Get up."

She rose slowly, not wanting to spook him.

"Which way?" he said.

"Upstairs."

"Let's go."

She felt the shotgun muzzle against her lower back. Wondered if she could turn fast enough, sweep it out of the way with an elbow, get ahold of the stock, pull it from his hands. But if it didn't work, she'd be gut shot or dead. And he wouldn't leave three witnesses to a murder. She needed to bide her time, keep her eyes open.

She went down the hall and up the stairs, the man close behind.

"So Cordell's dead," she said.

He poked her back with the shotgun.

"And his partner, too?"

"Shut up. Walk."

She went into Nancy's bedroom, pointed at the closet.

"Go on," he said.

She opened the sliding door, pulled the light cord. He stood a few feet behind her, the shotgun at waist level. She pushed clothes out of the way, reached up with both hands, got fingertips on the panel there, pushed it up and slid it over.

"Anything comes out of there except money," he said, "and your insides are going to be all over that wall."

She reached until she felt nylon, hooked one of the bag straps, pulled it toward her. She used both hands to bring the bag down out of the hole.

"Just the one?" he said.

"Just the one."

"Put it on the bed. Open it."

She unzipped the bag, pulled it open.

"Dump it out," he said. "Let's see what we've got."

They heard tires in the gravel driveway, saw headlights through the bedroom window. Roy coming back with the car.

She spilled the banded cash onto the bed, stepped back. He came closer, the shotgun still on her, picked up one of the money packs, fanned the bills with a thumb, dropped it back with the others.

"That looks about right," he said. "I'll take your word for how much is in there."

"That's all that's left."

"Put it back in the bag."

She replaced the money, zipped the bag shut. They heard the front door open.

He stepped forward, put the shotgun muzzle to the left side of her head. "I could do it now. Just like this."

"Then you'd have to kill all of us."

"I could do that, too."

In her peripheral vision, she saw his finger tighten on the trigger. She closed her eyes.

"Burke," Roy called from downstairs. "Where are you?"

"Asshole," Burke said under his breath. He took the shotgun away. She opened her eyes.

"Just fucking with you," he said. "Go on, get the bag."

She picked it up, went into the hall, felt him behind her as they went downstairs.

Roy was in the living room. He looked at the bag, said, "That it?"

Burke ignored him. He moved to one side, looking at Crissa, and she knew he was thinking it through, what to do next.

"You got what you came for," she said to him. "Take it. No one will come after you."

"That's the last thing I was worried about, to be honest," Burke said. "But you're right, it's just about the money, isn't it?"

"What are you saying?" Roy said. "You can't let her walk out of here."

"Anybody ask your opinion?" Burke said. He'd moved to Crissa's left, let the barrel of the shotgun drop. He was right-handed, so to fire he'd have to shift awkwardly, bring the gun around. It might give her the few seconds she needed.

"If it wasn't for me," Roy said, "you wouldn't—"

"Here," Crissa said. "You want it, take it." And threw the bag at Roy's face.

He reached up instinctively, caught it with both hands, and she moved in fast, yanked the Glock from his belt, shoved him backward, spun, and came up with the gun in a two-handed grip, pointed at Burke's chest.

The bag hit the floor. Roy fell back, tripped over the edge of the couch, landed on the carpet. Burke swung the muzzle of the Mossberg toward her. She held the front sight of the Glock on his chest, aiming for center mass, finger tight on the trigger.

They stayed that way for a long moment. Then Burke grinned.

"Well, here we go," he said. "You trust yourself to get a shot in before I take off your head?"

"I won't have to," she said. "My body will do it for me. A spasm in my finger'll be enough. At this range, I won't miss."

He shook his head, still grinning. Roy got to his feet.

"What I should have done," Burke said, "is just taken your head off the minute you walked in the door, then searched the house myself. Sooner or later, I'd have found the money, saved myself a lot of aggravation."

"Why didn't you?" Her finger tightened on the trigger.

"I don't know. Curious to talk to you, I guess. After everything I'd heard."

"Now you have."

"Do it," Roy said. "Shoot her."

"You could do that," she said. "But then you'd have a real mess to clean up, wouldn't you? And all you really want is the money."

"Don't listen to her," Roy said.

"There's your money right there," she said. "Take it. Walk away. Nothing's stopping you."

"I don't know if I can," Burke said. "After all the trouble you put me through."

"Would killing me make you feel better?"

"It might."

"Shoot her," Roy said.

Crissa took another step back, the gun steady.

"I don't know who you are," she said. "I don't know where you're going. You walk out that door, we'll never see each other again."

"You'd give it up just like that?" he said.

"Do I have a choice?"

"It's about these people, isn't it?" he said. "That little girl. Making sure they're okay. That there's no shooting in here. That's worth more to you than the money, right?"

She didn't answer.

Burke looked at Roy. "Do you believe this shit?" Then back at her. "You're everything I thought you'd be. I have to give you that."

"Take it," she said, and steadied her aim. "Walk away."

He let the muzzle of the shotgun drop an inch, said to Roy, "Pick it up."

"Don't believe her, man, don't—"

"Shut up. Pick it up."

Roy bent, hefted the bag.

"Take it out to the car," Burke said. "Wait for me."

"You can't leave her alive."

"Just do it. I'll be out in a minute." Roy looked at both of them, then turned, went quickly out the front, let the screen door slam behind him.

"Aren't you worried he'll take off with that money?" she said. "Leave you here."

"He won't."

She waited, the gun growing heavy in her hand.

"I was wondering," he said, "what the chances are of my taking that gun away from you."

"Not good."

"That's what I thought. And you're probably going to keep it on me until I'm out that door, right?"

She didn't answer.

He grinned again, started to back away, the shotgun still pointed at her.

"Maybe someday," he said, "we'll run into each other again."

He pushed the screen door open with his hip, lowered the shotgun, turned, and was gone.

She kept the gun pointed at the empty doorway. A breeze came through, pushed the balloon along the ceiling. She heard a car door open and shut, tires on gravel, the thump of a chassis as it bottomed out at the end of the driveway.

She let out her breath, let the Glock sag, went to the front door. Low mist covered the lawn. She watched taillights move off down the dark street, until the road curved and they were lost in the trees and fog.

The Glock felt like a lead weight in her hand. She walked the perimeter of the house to make sure they were gone, then went back inside. She stuck the gun in her waistband, pulled the tail of her sweater loose to cover it. Haley had seen enough guns tonight.

When she opened the door to the other room, Claudette

and Nancy were sitting on the bed, their hands cuffed in front of them. Haley was holding tight to her mother's arm.

"Is everyone okay?" Crissa said.

Nancy said, "Are they gone?"

"Yes." Crissa got out her penknife, cut through Nancy's flexcuffs.

"We have to call the police," Nancy said.

"No," Crissa said. "No police."

"Why not?"

Crissa looked at Haley, said, "Are you all right, honey?"

She nodded, said, "Help Mommy."

"I am," Crissa said, and cut through Claudette's cuffs. When her hands were free, she pulled Haley into her arms.

Nancy was rubbing her wrists. "Are you sure they're gone?"

"They're gone. I need you to find a motel for the three of you. Somewhere close by, just for tonight. Then I want you to call work, tell them you're sick, you had an emergency, whatever."

Nancy frowned. "Why?"

"Because I want things to seem as normal as possible. And I don't want anyone coming out here looking for you."

"Normal? Are you serious?"

"No one got hurt," Crissa said. "That's the important part. Please, just do as I ask. Get some clothes together, quickly. You all need to get out of here as soon as you can."

"Are they coming back?" Claudette said.

"I don't think so. I just want to be safe."

"Are you coming with us?" Nancy said.

"No," Crissa said. "I have some things to do first. I'll call you on that cell later. But you need to get moving."

When they were at the front door, overnight bags in hand, Haley in her mother's arms, Crissa said, "Wait a minute."

They looked back at her. She stood on her toes, reached, caught the string, pulled the balloon down from the ceiling. She carried it to Haley. "Don't forget this," she said.

Haley looked at it for a moment, then grasped the string. "Thank you."

"Remember, hold on tight," Crissa said. "Don't let it get away."

"I won't."

Crissa rubbed her back. "Go on now. I'll see you later."

She stood at the door, watched as they drove away. Then she took out the Glock, checked the magazine, saw it was full, a round in the chamber.

She went around the house, making preparations, turning out lights. Then she pulled on her gloves, sat down in the darkness to wait.

TWENTY-TWO

They were doing forty, the car seeming to ride on a carpet of mist, when Burke said, "God damn it!" and slammed on the brake.

The car slewed to the side, brakes screeching, came to rest half on the shoulder, headlights pointing off through trees. He'd narrowly missed the guardrail. There was a steep embankment beyond, then swamp.

"What the fuck?" Mapes said. He'd been counting the money in the open bag at his feet. Now the banded stacks were scattered on the floorboard.

Burke squeezed the wheel, looked out through the windshield, bit his bottom lip.

"What are you doing?" Mapes said. "Why are you stopping?"

Burke looked at him. "You don't get it, do you?"

"Get what?"

"She punked me back there. Punked me good."

"What's the difference? We've got the money, that's what we went there for, right?"

Burke slammed the shifter into park. There were no street-lights on this stretch of road, and they hadn't passed another car in ten minutes.

"It wouldn't bother you that, after all this, she's still walking around somewhere, would it?" he said. "After everything she did, all the shit she pulled?"

"But we got the money."

"Yeah, we did. Now put it back in the bag."

"How come?"

"It needs to go in the trunk. We can't be driving around with it up here."

When Mapes had the money in, the bag zipped shut, Burke said, "Get out of the car."

"Why?"

"Because I'm tired of your shit. I'm going to pay you off. Get out."

"Wait a minute. You can't leave me out here, middle of nowhere."

"Out."

Burke took the bag from him, got out, left the engine running. He went around to the trunk, opened it. Mapes got out of the car slowly. "Why are you wigging?"

"How much do you need?" Burke set the bag in the open trunk, unzipped it. "Is twenty enough?"

"What?"

"Twenty thousand. To cut you loose, leave you on your own right now."

"There's almost eighty in there."

"Doesn't matter. Your cut is twenty. You take it, then you start walking. About a mile or so back, you'll hit a place with some phones. You can call a cab."

"And what am I supposed to do then?"

"Up to you. But I'm done with you."

"Why do you have to be that way?"

"Twenty grand. Take it or leave it."

Mapes came up beside him. "I should get more."

"Right," Burke said, reached into the trunk, past the bag with the money, into the one beside it, drew out the Mossberg.

"Hey," Mapes said. "Wait—" and Burke brought the shotgun up between them, fired. It blew Mapes back, and Burke held the trigger down, worked the pump. The second blast knocked him over the guardrail and down the embankment.

Burke looked around. No headlights, no sign of a house nearby. He leaned over the guardrail, saw Mapes facedown in the wet grass, legs tangled. Too dark to go down there, check on him, make sure. He aimed at Mapes's motionless back, pumped and fired, pumped and fired. The noise echoed through the trees.

He put the shotgun back in the tac bag, shut the trunk lid on the money. Then he got behind the wheel, swung the car around in a wide U-turn, and headed back the way he'd come.

*　*　*

She was sitting on the couch, the Glock in her lap, when she heard the squeal of tires outside. Headlights swept across the living room.

She got up, went to the side window. He'd pulled up into the driveway, behind her rental, cut the engine. The headlights went out. She couldn't see him but heard the car door open, shut, footsteps on gravel. He was alone.

Just her car here now, as he'd expected. She'd sent the civilians away, was waiting inside for him, all the lights off. The backyard dark, too, where it had once been floodlit. Fog hung in the trees, but the sky was clear and full of stars, a half-moon shining.

He took the Browning from his belt, checked the magazine, the round in the chamber, clicked off the safety. He thought about taking the shotgun, but it wouldn't be right. Not this time.

He got out of the car, looked around. Two lots away to the west, the house there was dark. To the east, through a screen of trees, was another house, but only a single second-floor window showed light.

He started up the slate path.

She heard him coming, went to stand by the open door, the Glock at her side. She would only be a silhouette here through the screen door, a darker mass against a dark room.

He'd stopped on the path, maybe fifteen feet away, watching her, not moving, a gun at his side. Mist covered his feet.

"You surprised to see me?" he said.

She shook her head, even though she knew he couldn't see it. "No."

"All this time, all the miles I've come, you think I was just going to walk away like that?"

"You could have."

"Not me."

"Where's Roy?"

"Where do you think?"

"Was it worth it?" she said.

"What?"

"Everything." She waited, watching him, the gun in his hand.

"Honey," he said, "that's not the point." He brought the gun up and fired.

One second she was there, a dark shape in the doorway, outlined there, his finger tightening on the trigger, the gun jumping in his hand, and then she was gone.

It should have been an easy shot at this range. But he hadn't heard her fall or cry out. She was just there, and then she wasn't. The crickets had gone silent with the gunshot. After a moment, they started up again. He looked at the houses on both sides. No more lights had come on, no faces at windows. The fog had helped muffle the sound.

He lowered the gun, looking at the doorway. She had the

gun she'd taken off Mapes, but hadn't tried to return fire. She'd just turned away, gone deeper into the house, left him nothing to aim at but darkness.

"Son of a bitch," he said. If he wanted to follow her, end it, he'd have to go through that door, take his chances, knowing she was waiting on him somewhere inside.

He took a breath, looked at the car, thought about the money there in the trunk. It's all yours, he thought. All you have to do is drive away.

He looked back at the house. Still no movement inside. She was hiding somewhere in there, waiting on him, his decision.

"Fuck it," he said, and started for the door.

She heard him on the porch, heard the door open. She moved farther into the house, holding the Glock in both hands. In the hallway that led to the kitchen, she stopped, her back flat against the wall. The screen door shut, and she knew then he was inside. He'd come for her.

She ran.

He pulled the screen door open, pointed the gun into darkness, moved fast into the living room, finger tight on the trigger, looking for a target. The room was clear. The door shut behind him, and then a shadow broke from the others up ahead, moved fast down the dark corridor toward the kitchen. He took the shot, fired straight down that hallway, the muzzle flash bright.

He heard a gasp, and then the sound of the back screen door swinging open and slamming shut again. He ran toward the sound. Once out in the yard, she'd go for the trees, and then he might lose her. He had to end it before she got there.

He ran into the dark kitchen, feet skidding on the floor. He caught his balance, kicked the screen door open, pointed the Browning out into the yard, hit the light switch with his free hand. The floodlights went on, bathed the yard. Empty.

He looked down at his feet then, saw what he was standing on. Two shower curtains laid out on the floor, joined by a long strip of duct tape. Turning then, realizing the mistake he'd made, and there she was on the other side of the kitchen, the Glock in a two-handed grip, and he tried to bring his gun up, already knowing it was too late.

Her first shot hit him high in the chest, knocked him back against the screen door, surprise in his eyes. His gun came up, and she fired again, lower this time, correcting her aim. The third shot put him through the door and out onto the steps. A shell casing clattered into the sink behind her.

She let out her breath, watching for movement, her gun still up. Started slowly forward.

Burke looked up at the bright stars, the half-moon. He lay on cold concrete, his feet higher than his head, his gun gone. He couldn't move.

She filled the doorway above him, the gun still in her hands. He coughed, and there was blood in his mouth. He looked down at his chest, at the holes there, and saw a blood bubble rise from one of them. Sucking chest wound, he thought. Through the lungs. You're fucked.

He looked up again, saw a streak of light cross the sky and disappear into blackness. He tried to take another breath, but there was nothing there this time, just fluid. He looked at the moon, felt a coldness rise up inside him. Closed his eyes to meet it.

TWENTY-THREE

Crissa looked down at the man at her feet, the Glock pointed at his bloody, ruined chest. He lay on his back on the steps, eyes closed, his gun in the dirt a few feet away. She saw a red bubble rise from one of the holes in his chest. Then the bubble popped, and no more came after it.

There was no time to waste. She didn't know how far the sound of the shots had traveled. She set the Glock on the counter, then took his ankles, dragged him inside and fully onto the shower curtains. No blood on the concrete. She went past him and down the steps, got his gun and came back inside, set it next to hers. The air still reeked of gunpowder.

She flipped the wall switch, and the yard went dark. Kneeling, she touched a gloved finger to his carotid artery. No pulse.

She stood then, and her legs went weak. She reached a

chair, sat, drew air deep. The night was silent except for the crickets.

When she could trust herself to stand, she rolled him face-down onto the curtains, took out her penlight. She pulled the wallet from his back pocket, found his driver's license. Francis Xavier Burke, with an address in Detroit. She'd never heard of him. A couple of credit cards, a concealed-carry pistol license, fifty dollars in cash. In his jacket pockets were a pack of Newports, a silver lighter. That was it. She took the lighter, put everything else back.

Keep moving, she told herself. Don't stop to think.

His keys were in the car. With the headlights off, she swung the car around past hers, then reversed up the driveway and into the backyard.

When she opened the trunk, the sports bag with the money was in there. Below it were two tactical bags, and she saw they were matches for the ones Charlie Glass had gotten in Detroit. The first held guns, including the shotgun, and ammunition. The second was full of cash. She put all the money into the sports bag, filling it. She zipped it shut, carried it into the house, stowed it in a downstairs closet.

Using the penlight, she searched for shell casings. She found her three in the kitchen, another in the hallway. A final one on the slate path out front.

There was a spent slug on the hearth in the living room. It had gone through the screen door, the back of the couch, hit the fireplace mantel and bounced off to land mostly intact. She picked it up, then traced a path with the penlight beam along the hallway wall, saw the splintered trim where his second bullet had hit. With her penknife, she dug out the mush-roomed slug. She put it in her pocket with the casings.

Back in the kitchen, she rolled him into the curtains, bound them with duct tape. She took a breath, then dragged him out the door feet first, down the steps and into the dark yard. She was winded by the time she got to the car. It took all she had to get him up and into the trunk.

Time to move. She shut the trunk, got behind the wheel, went down the driveway with the headlights off, turned at the road. She heard the thump of something rolling in the trunk, braked to listen. It didn't come again.

She drove for a half hour, the mist reflecting the head-lights back at her. She passed through a town with a brightly lit shopping plaza, the lights haloed in the fog, then onto a long stretch of dark road alongside a river. At the first bridge she came to, she pulled onto the shoulder, put her hazards on and got out, looked over the concrete railing at the dark water below. She took the Browning and the Glock from her pockets, unloaded them, wiped them down with a handker-chief, then disassembled them by the light of the bridge stan-chion. Everything went into the water. She listened for each splash, then dropped in the shell casings and slugs.

She drove another ten minutes, found a dirt road that led out into woods. She took it as far as she could, until the road ended at a wooden barrier, nothing but darkness beyond. It would have to do.

She powered down the windows for ventilation, shut off the lights and engine, used her penlight to check the car a final time. She found a banded pack of cash under the passenger seat—five hundred dollars. She put it in a jacket pocket. There might be more in the trunk, but she wasn't going to open it again.

The swamp smell was strong here. She could hear water just beyond the barrier. She opened the rear door, used her penknife to slice through the seats, then pulled out chunks of cushioning. She took a road map from the glove compartment, ripped it into pieces, stuffed them down into the torn seats, then uncapped the can of charcoal lighter she'd taken from the kitchen. She doused everything, the acrid smell of the fluid rising up, dropped the empty can on the floor. The gas tank had been three-quarters full. It would be enough.

Way out here, with no lights around, the sky was bright with stars. The moon gave enough light that she could see the dirt road, the shape of trees on both sides. She could hear the bellowing of frogs, then the sound of something big moving through the water.

She tossed the keys out past the barrier, heard them splash, then used his lighter to set the map on fire, backed away as the flames rushed up the upholstery, licked at the back window. If it burned long enough, it would reach the trunk, then the gas tank. It was the best she could do. She started back up the road.

She'd just reached the main road when she heard the muffled explosion. She looked back, saw a glow through the trees, heard faint popping. The ammunition going up. She walked on.

A half hour later, she came to the bridge, dropped the cigarette lighter into the water. No cars on this road, but she could see the distant lights of the shopping plaza ahead. She'd find something open, call a cab, have it drop her a few blocks from the house. Go through the place again, looking for any traces Burke and Roy might have left. Then make that phone call.

She walked on under the stars, and tried not to think of what she'd done.

TWENTY-FOUR

"This is more than it was," Nancy said.

"Yes," Crissa said. There was an even hundred thousand in the sports bag now, rebanded and neatly packed. "Remember what I told you about banks."

They were in Nancy's bedroom, the bag open on the bed.

"And nobody's going to come looking for it?"

"Not anymore," Crissa said.

"What happened here last night, after we left?"

"Do you really want to know?"

Nancy looked at her, then at the money. "Part of me does. And part of me thinks I'm better off not knowing."

"Maybe that's best."

They could hear Haley outside, singing to herself. Crissa went to the window, looked out on the backyard. Haley was sitting on the rear steps, iPod in hand, earbuds in her ears, kicking her heels lightly against the concrete.

"She seems okay," Nancy said. "I was worried. But it's hard to tell. She doesn't talk much. She's trying to forget it all, is the sense I get."

"If she's lucky, she will."

"I'm going to have to keep an eye on her, talk with her if I can."

"You've got that cell," Crissa said. "And in a few days, I'll call, give you a PO box as well. Anything comes up, you need to reach me, you'll be able to."

"You're leaving?"

"Soon as I'm packed."

"I don't know what to say."

"You don't have to say anything." She zipped up the bag. "Just remember to be careful with this."

"I will."

"Take some of it, get Claudette into a program, a good one."

"We've already talked about it. She has a meeting with a counselor this week. I'm going with her."

"That's good."

"But I can't help wondering if Roy's going to show up again, drag her back down with him."

"Not this time," Crissa said.

She stowed her bag in the trunk of the rental, looked up the driveway to where Haley sat on a flat rock by the creek. She'd watched Crissa getting ready, packing her bag. Then she'd taken her iPod out to the creek, and hadn't come back.

Claudette came out of the house, over to the car. "Is this it? Are you going?"

Crissa shut the trunk. "You know how to reach me. If something comes up, I'll get back down here as soon as I can."

"You can stay, you know."

Crissa looked at her.

"As long as you want," Claudette said. "Nancy and I talked about it. It might be a good thing for all of us. You, too."

"Thanks, but I have places I need to be."

"Where?"

Crissa didn't answer.

"I'm not sure where you're going," Claudette said, "or exactly who you are, to be honest. But I want you to know that whatever happens, whatever trouble you run into, you'll always be welcome here."

Crissa nodded, looked up at the creek. Haley hadn't moved.

"Thanks for that," Crissa said. "I guess I'll say my goodbyes, get going."

She walked up the driveway, Claudette watching her. Haley was throwing pebbles into the water. She wore the Mickey Mouse T-shirt Crissa had bought her.

"Hey, angel."

Haley didn't turn.

Crissa sat beside her. "I wanted to say—"

Haley got up, walked fast to the house, ran the last few

feet. Crissa watched her go. The screen door closed behind her.

I don't blame you, Crissa thought. Hold on to that anger. You'll need it.

She went back to the car, got behind the wheel, started the engine.

Backing down the driveway, she saw Haley at the front door, looking through the screen, Claudette behind her.

She braked. The screen door flew open, and Haley came out running. Claudette stayed in the doorway.

Crissa got out of the car just as Haley reached the end of the path. She held her arms out, and Haley flew into them, hugged her, squeezing hard. Crissa squeezed back, felt her warmth, smelled her hair. She held her for a long time, neither of them speaking. Claudette stood behind the screen door, watching.

"Okay, angel," Crissa said. "Time for you to go back inside." Haley held her tighter.

Crissa reached behind, gently loosened her grip. "Your mom's waiting for you."

Haley let go, looked up, and Crissa waited for the question to follow. Instead, she turned away, started back up the path to the house. Claudette held the screen door open. Haley went inside, and Claudette looked back at Crissa, then followed her in. The door shut behind them.

Crissa got in the car, backed out onto the road, stopped there, looking at the house. Haley hadn't been crying. That little girl, she thought, is tougher than you think.

She headed up the coast road to I-95. She'd return the car

in Jacksonville, take Amtrak from there. In a little more than a day, she'd be home.

She drove on, took her sunglasses from the rearview, put them on. But it didn't help the stinging in her eyes.

TWENTY-FIVE

"I didn't expect to see you again so soon," Walt Rathka said.

She set the two Whole Foods bags on the floor by his desk. She could hear the traffic on Fifth Avenue, twelve stories below.

"Thought your diet could use a little improvement," she said. "More natural foods, less processed."

There were fruit and vegetables in both bags. Beneath them, a sheet of newspaper, then neat stacks of banded bills.

"I'm sure you're right," he said. He was in his late fifties, wore a dark suit with a blue club tie and suspenders. "Thanks for thinking of me. How natural?"

She took the seat opposite his desk, tapped her left ear.

"It's okay," he said. "Things have calmed down a bit. And

I'm having this place swept once a week now. It's expensive, but you can't put a price on peace of mind, can you?"

"No," she said. "You can't." She nodded at the bags. "One-sixty. Give or take."

He gave a low whistle. "In two weeks? I hope that didn't involve any unnecessary risk."

"Unexpected," she said. "But not unnecessary."

"Cryptic as always. And how fresh would these provisions be?"

"Very. Raw, actually. They could use a good washing."

"Ah," he said. "That's good to know. You have a preference as to the method?"

"Whatever needs topping off. But I want you to set up something else, too, another offshore account, with a monthly payout to a name and address I'll give you."

"Another one? How much?"

"Five hundred a month. For now."

"Five hundred," he said. "That adds up. You're being generous."

"But you can do it?"

"Take me a couple weeks, but I think I can get it going for you. How are things besides that?"

"Good enough," she said.

"That's not very convincing."

"It is what it is."

"Money to spend but nothing to spend it on?" he said.

"Something like that."

"Well, you're very practical-minded, I know. But if someday

you're interested in entering the world of fine art acquisition, let me know. I could make some suggestions."

She smiled. "I don't think so. It would be wasted on me. I wouldn't know the good from the bad."

"Who does? It's not about good and bad. Anyway, that's all relative."

"Isn't everything?" she said.

The man in the guayabera shirt put on his reading glasses, looked at the sheet of paper Crissa had given him. They were in the back office of a storefront insurance company in Jersey City. All the signs in the front window were in Spanish.

"I'll need another picture, of course," he said. "You want to take it now?"

"No. I'll come back tomorrow. I need to make some alterations first."

She set the thick manila envelope on the desk. "Same as last time. Half now, half when it's ready."

He sat back, took off his glasses. "*Señora,* I have no problem taking your money, you know that. And I'll always be grateful to my cousin Hector"—he crossed himself—"for introducing us. But I have to ask: The other two aren't good enough? You need a third?"

"You're an artist, Emilio. The best. But this one I want for a specific purpose, and one purpose only. And no passport this time, just a driver's license, birth certificate, and credit card. They need to hold up to a general background check, though, so they have to be solid."

He picked up the paper again. "I don't even know what a Texas license looks like. I'll have to do some research."

"I'm sure you can work it out."

He set his glasses on the desk. "I've never thought of you as a customer, *señora*. More as a colleague."

"Likewise."

"But I can't help be concerned. Every time I take on one of these, it increases our risk."

"That's what the money's for."

"*Si*. But it's not just about the money. When I worked for the DMV in Newark, I could run off licenses all day. No one cared as long as the supervisors got their cut. But these days, no one looks the other way. It's a federal thing. Prison, maybe."

"Risks we take."

"And you're only going to use it for one thing?"

"And one thing only," she said. "Four times a year. Five at most. Only one or two people will ever see it. I just need to keep it separate from the others. Those are for emergencies."

He nodded. "I'll do the best I can for you, Miss . . ." He looked at the paper. "Patrick?"

"That's right," she said.

"Shana Patrick, from Austin, Texas. That's a good Anglo name. I like that name."

"Let's hope it's a lucky one," she said.

TWENTY-SIX

The line moved slowly, the guard at the door checking IDs against the clipboard he held. There would be two more inside, a man and a woman, to do the pat-downs, search the strollers. She was tired from the flight, the drive down from San Antonio, and as the line moved forward, she felt the knot in her stomach tighten.

The blacktop was soft under her feet, the heat coming up through her sneakers. In front of her, a black girl barely out of her teens rocked the child she was holding. It was a little girl, maybe a year old, pink bows in her hair. She looked over her mother's shoulder at Crissa, reached. Crissa put out her hand, let the girl take her finger, squeeze. The mother patted the girl's back, turned to look at Crissa and smiled, and then the line was moving again.

When Crissa reached the guard, she handed over her driver's license without being asked. He took it, matched it against the names on the approved visitors sheet, said, "Cap and sunglasses."

She took off the baseball cap, stuck it in the back pocket of her jeans. Her hair was cut short, dyed black. When she removed her sunglasses, the guard held the license up to her face, looked at both, and handed the license back to her without a word.

Inside, a female guard patted her down, pointed to a Plexiglas window with a metal shelf. There was a desk beyond the glass, a black woman there talking on the phone. On the shelf was the spiral ledger that served as the visitors log. There was a cheap plastic pen beside it, taped to a piece of string tied to one of the spirals.

The room was already half full. Mostly women, mostly black or Hispanic, small children in tow. Black and white checkered floor, vending machines against one wall. Cameras high in every corner. Two guards at the door and two more standing around, watching.

She signed the log the way she'd practiced. A guard pointed her to an empty table in a corner. The table and benches were all bolted down. She sat with her back to the wall, facing the security door on the other side of the room. Sunlight came through the window above and behind her, lit dust motes in the air. She put her sunglasses back on, closed her eyes.

She tried to slow her breathing, listened to the noises around her. The security door opening and closing, soft conversations in Spanish, babies crying. But she was drifting. In her mind was the glow of a fire in night woods, muzzle flashes in a dark kitchen.

She heard the security door buzz open, felt him before she saw him. She opened her eyes, and he was standing there in front of her, black hair combed back, streaked with silver, more than she remembered, a lopsided grin. She took off her sunglasses.

"Hey, darlin'," he said.